Bertha De Jongh

The Sisters Lawless

A novel

Bertha De Jongh

The Sisters Lawless
A novel

ISBN/EAN: 9783337052461

Printed in Europe, USA, Canada, Australia, Japan

Cover: Foto ©Andreas Hilbeck / pixelio.de

More available books at **www.hansebooks.com**

THE SISTERS LAWLESS.

A Novel.

BY THE AUTHOR OF "ROSA NOEL."

"For in every breast that liveth
Is that strange mysterious door;—
The forsaken and betangled,
Ivy-gnarled and weed-bejangled,
Dusty, rusty, and forgotten." . . .

IN THREE VOLUMES.
VOL. I.

LONDON·
RICHARD BENTLEY AND SON.
1874.

THE SISTERS LAWLESS.

CHAPTER I.

FATHER AND SONS.

ITTLE Mrs. Lawless had an idea
that it sounded more loving
to call her relations something
which ended in "ie," than to give them
their full first names. So her sister
Rosalind changed into Rosie, her brother
Elphinstone became Elphie, and after she
married, her husband, Francis, never got
his real name from her, but was Frank or
Frankie; appellations peculiarly unsuited
to him, since he was dark, and rather
sinister looking.

Her first-born having been christened

Bertrand, Mrs. Lawless naturally called him Bertie; and from her pink lips the fine name of the second son, Adrian, dwindled into the paltry and comic diminutive, Adie.

For a third son, several years younger than Adrian, poor little Mrs. Lawless had not time to fix on a pet name, for she died soon after he was born. Fox he was christened, and Fox he was called to his last day. Of course, if his poor, pretty mother had lived, he would have been Foxey.

Between his first day and his last, he was sorely chastened, for he was lame, hopelessly lame, and with the sensitive, exacting, quick-perceiving, shrewdly-judging mental condition that one frequently finds in the crippled, or in those whom Providence has seen fit to deprive of one pain and delight giving sense.

Fox was a pretty fellow; hazel-eyed, and chestnut-haired, with hands white and slender as a woman's. His teeth sparkled from under the sweetest, most curling upper lip in the world, when he spoke, while his brown eyes had the perplexed and troubled gravity of one who has never tasted the bright realities of youth.

Weak and delicate, doomed never to run and leap, nor to bestride man's beautiful four-footed servant, nor to enjoy any of boyhood's active, joyous games, Fox Lawless, probably, derived as much satisfaction from life, in the long run, as did his two stalwart elder brothers, to whom, in the matter of description, precedence should properly have been given, for it is with them that our story has mostly to do.

Bertie, the eldest, verges on eight and twenty; he is Adrian modified and embellished. Shorter, slighter, fairer, with deep, gray eyes, and hair that is pure, ungilded brown; he is slender, agile, deft with his hands, light on his feet, the treasure of his cricket club, the gem of football players at Harrow, when he was a few years younger. See him on his little yacht, and you would say that he was born to be a sailor; watch him bestride his horse, and gallantly ride as the crow flies and you would vow that pity 'twas Fate had not ordained him a place lower in the social scale, that the turf might claim him as the jockey of jockeys. See him vault that high railing, and the conviction would be yours, that in acrobatic feats, he would have made a mark and a fortune. He is frank and light hearted. He is charming. You admit it before you have spoken to him for ten minutes. You endorse your own opinion of him the second time you meet him, and you go on endorsing it, to the end of your acquaintance with him.

Adrian, a year younger, is darker, taller, less charming, and far less handsome than his brother. The first time you see him, he strikes you as being repellent. As you talk with him, however, you find that he says what you want him to say at the right moment, that he is quick to take half-expressed meanings; as you get to know him better, you discover that he glows under kindness, and blazes under cavalier treatment, that there is no smoulder of vindictiveness, no chill of surly resentment, no magpie hiding of revengeful intentions in all his liberal nature. He would be an honest friend, and a clear sighted ; a fair foe, and a warm lover enough.

Down in one of the southern counties is Creyke Park. The old house stands staring out at the thick timber surrounding it, with many window eyes, innocent of plate glass ; modern improvements not being the order of the day at Creyke. There are no artificial lakes, no orchid houses, aviaries, few flowering shrubs and specimen trees. What picturesque walks there are, have been made by nature, unassisted by the owner of Creyke.

The park palings are in many places broken and dilapidated, the lodge-gates have a look of powerful old age, and the ivy graciously covers the short-comings of the lodges themselves.

Inside the house there was a strange confusion of majolica bowls and decrepit furniture, of cloisonné enamel caskets, and cracked Queen's ware, of deal tables and midiæval chests of drawers, of art treasures and of trumpery. The dining-room was the worst room of all, and in it, on a February morning, winterish and gray, the brothers were seated at break-fast. It was a room to shudder at always, and to become attached to never. Horse hair, abominably slippery and unpleasant, covered its furniture. A towering screen, ornamented with every conceivable scratch and daub, in the shape of ill-coloured, ill-drawn print and engraving (the pasting on of which had been one of the late Mrs. Lawless's life works), stood by the fire-place, where smouldered the smallest, most sullen of fires. Grim men and women of the tribe of Lawless, stared and scowled from the walls. Even the pic-tured children, who had once borne the name of Lawless, had the determined family knitting of the brows. No smile brightened one of the fat, baby faces. With an admirable gravity, they caught the eye of the spectator with their own dark and solemn ones, and the spectator was fain to turn discomfited away.

There was a buffet of great antiquity and ugliness between the windows, and this, with an old sofa, the table, and the necessary chairs, comprised the furniture.

The young men were breakfasting in almost complete silence. Fox was playing at eating, while his two elder brothers gratified a most substantial appetite. Shortly, the door opened, and the master of the house made his appearance, and, rubbing his thin, gentleman's hands together, to chafe the chill of a fireless room, gave some unintelligible word of greeting. He seated himself at the table, but in a moment he was up again, and going to the fire, he tried to coddle it into burning slower, by making a little cover of ashes for it. He returned, and taking his chair, looked eagerly down at the scanty breakfast, longing for it to be less not more.

It was quite five minutes before he spoke; then he said, "A week from to-day, Maria. Three weeks from to-day the young women, the nieces, your cousins, boys. There will be—ha—*some* changes necessary for them ; I am very far from saying many, or great changes. Ties of blood, ties of blood, are—ha—a——"

" Nuisance," struck in Fox.

" I was very far from saying that," returned his father, " very far indeed—a tax I might be allowed, even by the most censorious, to consider them ; yes, two young women who must have a chaperon ; another tie of blood, another tax ; my sister Maria is poor, she tells me, so am I, so am I ; the rents are irregular in coming, things are out of joint with me always, I am a poor man, a very poor man, with no hope of ever being a richer one."

He paused, with a stealthy upward glance from under his thick brows at his three sons, who in their various ways showed a natural, if unfilial impatience, and a half-veiled scepticism as to their father's words.

" No ; no hope of ever being better off, unless one of my sons is a fortunate son, or an enterprising, and a clever, and an able. A happy thing—ha—to have a fortunate

child, a sort of family success. Adie, how
goes it with you in town ? scope, eh ? opportunity ?"

" Perhaps," answered the young man,
"for anybody equal to the occasion, anybody with the proper capacity for law work.
The fact is, father, I believe that to have
been a success I should have come here a
few centuries earlier. I ought to have
been a Troubadour; I'm sure that I could
have touched a guitar gaily—very gaily ;
and I look the character, don't you think ?"
He rose from the table as he spoke, laughing, expanding his broad chest, and stretching out his athletic arms.

His father observed him with dissatis-
faction ; evidently in his belief the moneyed
success of the family was not personated by
his second born.

To Bertie, who was still crunch-
ing crisp toast, he now turned. Bertie,
the beauty, the inverately lazy one—
he turned to him. Bertie persistently
acted the part of fine gentleman, and
idled at home, running into debt whenever
it suited his convenience, and handing in

his unpaid bills to his father, in a very
jaunty and engaging way, from time to
time.   Bertie owned a small cutter yacht,
had a fine saddle horse in the dilapidated
old stable, was not without a gratified taste
for jewellery, and was altogether the most
obstinate of drones. Mr. Lawless addressed him with a sneer. " The beau,
the buck, the butterfly, Bertie, will be, ha—
the successful spendthrift of the family ; is
your yacht paid for, Bertie ?"

" No."

" Your horse ?"

" No ; pay for them when you please,
father, Lewis and Franks are perfectly
willing to wait ; they don't mind ; the
money will be forthcoming some day or
another, they rest assured.   Yes, I'll be the
successful spendthrift of the family with all
the pleasure in life," he went on gaily, and
with a most melodious laugh, " I want no
better employment, it suits every inch
of me."

His father struck his still strong and
white teeth together with a sudden, sharp

click ; his every feature betraying a violent irritation, a very fever of vexation, for Bertie's unconquerable extravagance was a grievance, sore and of long duration.

Bertie hastily concluding his breakfast, made a rush for the door, eager to escape, and running through the hall, inhaled the clear winter outside air with the keenest relish. Mr. Lawless's long, meagre, mean chin sunk upon his breast. His pinched nostrils, with their crafty elevation at the end nearest the cheek, grew more depressed, as he watched his eldest son's departing form.

Adrian, too, watched his brother, but with what inner comment is not known, for the clear tones of Fox, who had been silently regarding them both, were now heard, and they said unconcernedly: "What a bitter bad failure I am, father, ain't I ?"

Mr. Lawless screwed up one shoulder to meet his ear, elevated his eyebrows, and drew down the corners of his mouth without replying in words.

"Wait," Fox went on. "Some day I

may make myself famous by 'blood or
ink '———"

"When do you mean to begin?" demanded his father in a tone of depressing facetiousness, of mournful pleasantry.

"I am waiting," said Fox, "for the ig-
nition of that furor poeticus, which I am
convinced I possess."

The boy leaned back, as he finished
speaking, clasping his thin hands together
under his head.

His father waved his hand; "There,
poor boy, go back to your fairy tales, go
back to your Waverley novels! Nothing is
expected of you—ha—nothing—our chast-
enings are good for us, yes, no doubt."
He paused, then went on, "But the trial
that can least stand alone, is poverty—
want of means. Death and disgrace are
both bad, very bad; but we weather 'em
if we have money; yes, we live 'em down;
but poverty we can't live down, no, it
starves us out, it pulverizes us, it brings
with it a numerous progeny of evils that the
other afflictions somehow don't seem able

to collect. It has a terrible beak and claws, want; it is an able assistant to the inherent vileness of the human heart; it brings out crime as rain does the earth worms, as a clear sky, the stars, as a match to powder brings an explosion— yes."

"Apt," said his youngest son under his breath, "fine illustrations, glowing similes !"

His father did not hear. Wrapt in meditation, he sat motionless long after Fox had taken his crutch and limped out of the room to his usual haunt, the library; and Adrian had gone to pack, or rather to pitch, his effects into a portmanteau preparatory to going up to town, and waiting amongst spiders, must, cobwebs, law-books, and comfortable furniture, for his maiden brief.

He disliked his profession, and those cramped rooms of his, looking out upon house-tops infested by predatory cats— who found, poor things, little enough to prey upon !—his very soul loathed.

Bertie, meanwhile, had sauntered out into the moist, cold air, and had betaken himself to the stables, where his mare, scenting his approach, gave him a welcoming whinny.

He entered her loose box, stroked her velvet coat, and telling the stable boy to saddle her, stood watching the operation, and at its conclusion mounted the thing he loved best in the world, and went clattering away over the paved stable-yard, and out a ramshackle gate.

He wore a black necktie, and black gloves, out of respect to his uncle, who, nine months ago, had finished his earthly campaign.   An uncle not in the least known to him ; for, many years ago, Charles Lawless had been ordered to Canada with his regiment, and, although in due course the regiment had returned, he had not, for he sold out, and established himself in the quaint and mean Lower Canadian town of St. Dominic, with his wife and two daughters.   His wife had died a few months after his arrival, leaving these two children, separated in age by a gap of four years. At this present, therefore, the eldest was two and twenty, the younger but eighteen.

Very speedily they were to leave their home, and come out to their natural guardian and protector, their father's elder and only brother, Francis Lawless of Creyke Park.

With what glee their advent was anticipated, we have seen a little. Perhaps of the four Bertie dreaded them least ; his was a blithe, and insouciant temperament, prone to depict future events in bright tints rather than dark, and to have dismal presages concerning very few things this side of the grave.

Two young lady-cousins domiciled within the gray walls of Creyke, seemed to him an agreeable variation of the ordinary quarrel-infested home-life. He chirruped to his horse as he reached the main road, and cantered gaily away.

CHAPTER II.

FIELD of cloth of silver, a sky of sapphire, a radiance of sunshine unsurpassable; a still, and glittering, and lonely scene, and bitter, ah *bitter* cold.

A winter landscape in Canada; an expanse of ermine snow stretching to right and left as far as eye can see; an air so motionless that not the smallest twig is stirred; a sunlight that dazzles, here and there making some sharp icicle emit prismatic rays, or throwing off from a heaped drift such a glare of frozen white light, that one involuntarily contracts one's eyebrows and eyelids.

What odd marks are these, indenting the crisp and polished surface of the snow ? Are they foot-prints of two strange enormous-claw'd birds ? .

Follow them along the lonely tract, skirting the frozen and marble river, over the beautiful desolate white fields, and we presently overtake their cause—two women's figures, tall, and slender also in spite of their fur jackets and thick woollen skirts. They are snow-shoeing ; plodding, foot over, foot under, in the unimaginably awkward gait that must be the snow-shoer's, be she graceful as any fawn at more ordinary slippered times. Their little fur caps are pulled low on their foreheads, and wound about throat, mouth, and nose, are fleecy white woollen wrappings, over which their two pairs of eyes peep, as if they were cherubically surveying life over a cloud.

" Angela," the taller of the two is saying, " it is a dangerous month to cross."

" If you were philosophical you would find all months dangerous alike for the matter of that," returned the other with a muffled laugh.

"But I am not philosophical, and I prefer crossing the ocean in a month that is not proverbially stormy. If I cannot make you think of the danger—and I know I cannot—think of the discomfort. Do you remember when we came out? Everything movable seemed gifted with more than human, with impish vivacity, and power of locomotion. Do you recollect how mamma's coil of false hair wriggled off like a snake, and was found in the cabin of the old gentleman opposite? And how boots and shoes, seizing the opportunity, eloped with their neighbour's mates, and were never more found?"

"I have misty memories of a chaotic two weeks," was the reply.

What contrasts were the two voices. The last speaker never changing her key, or elevating her voice, or emphasizing in the least degree, the other, full of swift and harmonious changes, of varieties of tone, of deep notes, and silvery.

There was a pause broken only by the scratch, scratch of snow-shoes.

" How do you think we shall like our baby-faced cousins ?" the last speaker began again.

" How do you know that they are baby-faced ?"

" Of course they are. Could the names Adie and Bertie belong to anything that had not a baby face ?"

" How can I tell ?"

" *I* can tell. Instinct assures me that any truly manly man would have freed himself from the odium of a name like either of those."

" I am not instinctive any more than I am philosophical, and I could remind you, Angela, of dozens of people to whom nursery names have clung, and will cling as long as they live. The hardest thing in the world to get rid of, is a nick-name. What a shame it is to give children nick-names, for they are generally either ugly or silly sounding."

" Clemence, a man of parts (am I not

quaint?) would have thrown off such a name as Adie, directly he was out of his teens; not that it matters in the least to us; but I do so hate to bully; and I must bully these feeble ones, I know I must. How unkind circumstance is to us, what scope is given us, what tempting opportunity for the display of our pet, yet most self-condemned, faults. You know how domineering I am—I say it is unkind of Fate to throw me at the head of two inevitable victims."

"Why unbridle your imagination, Angela? There is nothing inevitable——"

" Spoken like myself!" cried her sister tapping her approvingly on the shoulder with her muff; "right, my commonplace one, quite right—don't finish your sentence, leave it accidentally epigrammatic."

The elder girl laughed good temperedly, and in a few minutes their plodding had brought them into the principal street of a queer old French Canadian town, where shrill French voices prevailed, and

shrivelled cedar-coloured French faces pre-
dominated.

St. Dominic was dirtier than it was dull,
and uglier than it was dirty. Now, it
showed a fair front, being smoothly
covered with snow, until it was white and
shining as a wedding-cake. Low carrioles,
often with the fur robes trailing out at the
side and making a glittering white dust as
they drag along, come at a perilous speed
down the narrow steep street, drawn by
rough ponies with long fetlocks and wild
eyes, and driven by muffled men or women,
of whose faces nothing but the eyes is
visible, giving a baffling and mysterious
look to them, as they rush past. Sometimes a rough sledge tears by, the French
Canadian driver standing upright on it,
giving a wild cry, as he urges his horse
down into a cahot, and up again ; his bells
jingling madly, as he plunges down into
the snowy hollow. The whole air is filled
with the sound of sleigh-bells ; chiming in
with one another with something like har-
mony, clashing discordantly with one

another; or—but this happens rarely—tinkling out merrily alone.

The western sun glints on the pressed-down, polished surface of the snow, and along the smooth lines that the last runners have left, makes a track like a little straight, flat-lying rainbow.

Arrived at the porch of a quaint-looking little house, the sisters slipped off their snow-shoes, and in their four pairs of stockings apiece, and their soft doe-skin moccasins, entered the house with velvet footsteps : the elder gaily humming a tune, the younger in silence.

A blazing fire welcomed them, and wooed the red blood to the cheeks of the elder sister; to the younger, it brought only a pink, pale as the blossom of the Canada thistle, which brightened her face for three minutes and then fled. They went upstairs to their rooms, talking together in their usual diversity of style and voice and manner. Dinner, with the two young faces opposite one another, the two dissimilar appetites (Angela's so dainty,.

Clemence's so hearty), was quickly de-
spatched, and a long evening came, like
unto many and many another that had gone
before it.

They drew their chairs close by the
blazing coal, and for ten minutes neither
spoke. It was the elder who broke the
silence.

" Angela, a new phase of life is about
to begin for us——"

" Clemence," interrupted the other, with
the usual half tolerance which marked her
tone when addressing her sister, " don't
be fantastic in your wording of commonplaces ; it doesn't suit you. We are going
to our uncle in England, yes ; away from
these odious patois talkers with their
wooden faces and raisin eyes, and thankful
am I. I long for to-morrow morning that
I may, with some pretence of necessity,
begin packing, and feel that I am placing
the fact I long for safely outside my imagination. I am so imaginative, Clemence.
You, with your clock's precision and quietude, could not realize what flights my

fancy takes when you are sound asleep,
and breathing those enormously long
breaths that I often think are never coming
to an end ; so—Clemence—— " with an
exaggerated respiration.

" I do sleep very soundly," replied
Clemence, apologetically, " but do you
know," she hesitated and paused, " I have
sometimes waked and heard you—snoring."

" Snoring ?" repeated her sister, with
unfeigned indignation ; " I snore, Clemence ? what life-like dreams you must
have !"

" Very life-like indeed," Clemence answered, with her delightful, rippling laugh ;
" very much so, indeed, Angela, dear ; but
don't frown at me like that—look in the
glass, and see how unbecoming it is to
you."

Angela, on the instant, sprang from her
chair, and taking great pains to keep her
expression unchanged, gazed, rapt, at herself in the mirror between the windows.

" It does not suit me," she said, thoughtfully, and thereupon smoothed her countenance into its usual charming placidity.

Being a skilful and experienced pilot among the rocks and shoals of her sister's humours, Clemence steered direct for another, and undoubtedly safe topic.

"Angela," she said, looking at her with the wholesome admiration of one pretty woman for another, "what a pretty surprise you will be to them. I do hope the sea-voyage will not have left its ugly traces upon you."

"I hope not, I am sure," coincided Angela, with fervour ; "but don't they say that it makes one doubly fair and clear to be very ill at sea ?"

"Oh, a long time afterwards," returned the other, shaking her head, but adding cheerily, warned by the real consternation depicted on her sister's face, "the pretty time will come after we have been there a while. Now let us have tea."

She turned as she spoke, and with extreme care poured out her fastidious sister's post-prandial cup, and helping herself in a manner far more hasty, drew up again to the fire, satisfying herself with the draughty corner, while Angela snuggled up against a protecting curtain on the other side.

It was easy to guess that the all-absorbing theme of thought and conversation with them just now, was their approaching exodus from the only home they had ever known. Angela began at once :

" I have superb fancies of an old English home," half-closing her eyes, and looking very imaginative, " avenues of stately trees, with groups of startled deer beneath them. Mullions (what *are* mullions ?), gables, ivy, old armour, old servants, terraces with urns, rooms with names, old portraits (one of which I am sure to be like), family jewels, family trees, dogs that have grown old in the service, a staircase black and slippery with age and care—and all the rest of it," she wound up, waving her hand exhaustively. " I want to be gone."

" It is all very right and nice to go," answered the elder sister, with a shade of hesitation and doubt in her full, clear tones, "but it is leaving *home* after all; and, Angela, don't you think that you *may* be imagining a place far grander than we have any reason to suppose Uncle Francis' will be ? I somehow—don't——"

Angela interrupted her.

" Don't dishearten me. If you are commonplace, you can at least be sympathetic ; do be sympathetic. Why are you so willing to pother among the sordid realities of life, when you might as easily soar to fine, agreeable objects of—of— elevation ? You know how easily discouraged I am ; you know how vividly I picture future events to myself, and you delight in rubbing out my pictures with your matter-of-fact hands."

"Oh, Angela," cried Clemence, laughing, " oh, Angela, no one is more unwilling than I am to chill you by my—well, as you say—my commonplaces. But, dear, I should so hate for you to be disappointed; I should so hate for you to find that the contrast presented by your future to your

past home—this home—was less sharp
and complete than you had fancied it
would be. I am sure I hope as much as
you possibly can do, that Uncle Francis'
place is beautiful, and exactly what one
pictures———"

"You never picture anything," said
Angela, with a pout. "You wait for
things to jump down your throat. You
never exercise your mind in that prettiest,
most fantastic of ways, building Castles in
Spain."

"No I don't," assented Clemence,
honestly; "aërial architecture is not in the
least my metier."

Then she drew up to the table, and
engaged herself in calculations of how to
spread out their tiny income very thin,
that it might last until they sailed. Angela read a page of poetry, and then,
closing her eyes, dreamed a page of most
mawkish prose—opened them, and read
another page, and so on until the clock
struck ten, and being weary—snow-shoeing
is tiring play, and they had snow-shoed

long and far—the two sisters rose from
their different employments and betook
themselves gladly to bed.

On the Liverpool dock, stand two
figures, battered, wobegone, almost un-
tidy, and quite limp. Can these be the
two trim damsels, who, twelve days ago,
departed from Portland ; one, in tears for
her old home, that notwithstanding its
meagreness, its dinginess, she loved, the
other like a wild bird escaped from a cage?
Even so. Angela and Clemence step on
English ground for the first time since
babyhood.

"They might have sent a servant or
some one, to meet us," said Angela dole-
fully as she drooped over her large box,
and waited for the custom-house official to
examine it. "How can we ever go from
here to Barport alone ?"

"Perfectly well," rejoined Clemence
reassuringly. "I am such a tall, big,
strong-minded looking person——"

"Fortunately !" interpolated her sister

assentingly, and drooping more like a willow than ever.

"Come here," she cried appealingly to
the custom-house officer, "look into my
box, oh, pray do, and let us go."

The man, touched by her piteous accents,
her paleness, and her fair, angelic hair,
turned from his intended examination of
another box —the property of a sexless
looking person in spectacles, and a water-
proof down to its heels—and raising the
top of the box which Angela hastened
to unlock, apprised himself of a crape collar, an ivory Prayer-book, and some black
gloves, and professing himself satisfied,
marked the box, and went on his way,
followed by Angela's faint thanks.

Without tarrying at any hotel, the sisters
took train, and proceeded immediately on
their journey southwards, and, without let
or hindrance on the way, arrived duly at
the station where they would be, towards
five o'clock on a blustering March afternoon. A waggonette awaited them ; their
luggage lying where it was, to be taken up

a bit later on. The waggonette was seedy and unkempt; the horses harnessed to it, seedier and more unkempt.

Angela's bright blue eyes clouded, her sensitive mouth drooped ominously. The luxurious carriage, the attentive footman, and perhaps a baby-faced cousin or two coming to meet her, remained unrealities of her imagination, whose offspring they were. They clambered in, with only the assistance of a railway porter, who thereby expected a shilling, and got it; and the cadaverous, badly-got-up old coachman, perceiving slowly that they were in, and the door closed, slashed his horses awake, jerked up their heads, that had been drooping in senile slumber, and they jogged away.

Clemence watched her sister with concern. Angela, pouting, and sulky, and cruelly disappointed, gazed moodily, and in silence, over the wintry landscape of wet pasture land, field and copse, and labourer's cot. The sight of the handsome old gates through which they prepared to turn, warmed again in her heart the self-pleasing notions that had become chilled and dubious. She bent eagerly forward, and looked along the damp avenue with its rows of trees and shrubs growing suffocatingly close together, and its scanty red gravel.

Shortly, they drew up before the door, which upon its dull old front bore traces of having gone unvarnished for many a long year; the sun had blistered it, the damp had dimmed it. It was opened with a slowness and stealthiness quite ludicrous, seeing that they were two to be admitted, who should be inmates for an indefinite time.

"Ugh!" shuddered Angela, alighting, "this is depressing."

They entered, and from a neighbouring door, emerged a woman's figure, which advanced to meet them with something approaching a stiff stride.

"How do you do, Clemence and Angela?" said an unsympathetic voice in measured accents. "I would have come to meet you, but that I was not at all sure which train you would come by. I am glad to see you, my dear girls."

" This is Aunt Maria, I suppose ?" said Clemence in her deep, rich tones.

" Yes, Aunt Maria," responded the other, and led the way into a small sitting-room, where a large fire was making a fierce struggle to blaze out from under its crust of ashes. (Mr. Lawless gave directions about these ashes to the housemaids.)

There were dark shelves running along three sides of the room filled with china of Mrs. Lawless's collecting (for this had been her special retreat) china that was mostly trumpery, and that no connoisseur would have given house room, and that here, was a disfigurement rather than an adornment.

Over the mantelpiece hung the representation of a large, languishing blue eye ; one of Mrs. Lawless's eyes—or a likeness of it—which she had caused to be painted with an overwhelming sense of having done something startlingly novel, and

original ; eccentric to the verge of genius
in fact.

There it hung ; smiling at every in-
comer, from out its wide and massive
gilt frame.

Angela regarded it with unmixed horror,
and turned her back upon it, as if it had
been gifted with sight, poor painted
thing.

" Your uncle," said Miss Maria, hastily
ensconcing herself in her favourite chair,
fearful lest either of the two girls should
appropriate it unawares,—" is at Barport,
and will only be back in time for dinner, sit
down ; throw off your jackets, and hats and
tell me of yourselves ; tell me, in fact, all
about yourselves ; and then I will ring for
Martha to show you your rooms."

" What a friendly, not to say aunt-like,
proceeding is this !" thought Angela ;
" why could she not take us up herself,
and at once ?"

Angela had yet to learn her aunt's short-
comings. They were not of the sort that
elude detection, and are only known by

careful observation ; they came to the fore, and were soon seen. Determination never to have indigestion was one ; for, ruthlessly, Miss Lawless sacrificed the comfort and convenience of other people to those requirements which she considered necessary to the preservation of her now faultless gastric juice. The art of throwing dust in her own eyes was another ; a great fear of losing her own little superfluities of ease and luxury another ; and they did not end here. She was one of those uncomfortable people who are rich for themselves, and poor for everybody else. She was too, one of those uncomfortable people who make that ill-used word duty, a shield and buckler against very many of the ills of life. The ingenuity displayed by Miss Lawless in the self-advantageous use (or abuse) of the noble word, the dignity with which she entrenched herself behind it, would have been amusing if there were not something sad, always, in calm self-deception.

Angela, contracting her brows like a

very short-sighted person (which she was not), surveyed her new relative closely. She saw a woman of medium height, substantially well-formed; she saw a dark face with a coarse skin, a nose inclined to be retroussé, and a long tight upper lip; black eyes with very thin lids, and no under eye-lashes; black hair elaborately arranged. She was dressed in very slight mourning, and when she moved, her garments rustled like the garments of ten.

After kissing them, or rather, after allowing them to bend their tall heads and kiss her, Miss Lawless looked at her nieces with interest and curiosity. She found her elder niece to be a tall, and large-framed young woman, with dark, rich hair growing low upon her forehead, deep Irish gray eyes, and a very lovely mouth.

Angela seemed to her a thread paper thing, with enormous, glittering blue eyes, and a quantity of pale silken hair in curious, and unbecoming confusion.

For an hour the three talked together;

relating, asking questions, making family revelations.

Then Miss Lawless rose to touch the bell, but Clemence, springing up, rang it for her, with her long white fingers ; fingers how different from Miss Lawless's ten square-tipped, broad, digits ! Miss Maria's blood showed in her hands, truly, for they were of a most rural red. That they were so, and that not all the polissoirs, and poudre pour les ongles, would give her pretty nails, was a trial in chief to her. If Miss Maria had been put on oath to tell you what she most desired in life, she would answer, " Half-moons."

" Tell Martha to show Miss Lawless and Miss Angela their room," she said to the servant who answered the bell. " You have but one room," turning to the sisters, " we thought that you would probably be in the habit of occupying the same room, two sisters so often are."

" We have not been," said Angela, in her listless tones, " except now and again for fun, or when we have been nervous.

It doesn't matter ; indeed, perhaps it is better that we should, for I am sure to be nervous; come, Clemence. What time does my uncle dine ? I suppose we shall be busy in our rooms—room—until dinner-time."

"We dine at seven," replied Miss Maria, taking up her novel from where it lay, upon its face, and grasping a large gold-mounted flacon of eau de cologne. As the door closed upon her nieces, she fixed her lacklustre eyes upon her interrupted tale, and applied eau de cologne vigorously to her jaw-bone, for she was suffering from a tooth-ache.

"Clemence, Clemence," said Angela rue-fully, when they had entered their room, " this is not what I expected !" She sank down upon a hard, upright-backed chair, and looked dolorously at her sister, who answered the glance with a bright con-soling smile.

"How often things that begin uncom-fortably, end comfortably, Angela, dear," she replied.

"Why don't you say at once, a 'bad

beginning makes a good ending,'" said Angela crossly. " Those homely ' saws were made for you, I really believe."

" Come," cried Clemence, with some spirit, " get up, and help me to unpack, for it is only fair that you should, they are evidently not going to send any one to us. I will lift out all the heavy things, but indeed you must do your share in folding some of them away."

" I shall be afraid to go in there, even in the day-time," answered Angela, pointing to a cupboard door with a wizened little old key drooping out of its keyhole.

Clemence's only reply was to fly to the door, and, jerking it open, retreat a step or two, and survey its old pegs, hooks, and shelves.

" *Now* will you be afraid ?" she said in her clear and cheery tones.

" N—no," rejoined Angela, " oh, no, not now." And she thereupon proceeded to afford her sister some languid help, such as carrying away *one* collar, and shutting it up alone in a drawer, bearing off a porcelain box of hair-pins, and on her way to the dressing-table, stopping to extract one or two wherewith to pin up her recreant locks.

Angela's assistance was the most purely nominal thing possible, yet both sisters seemed to be satisfied, and as the dinner hour was on the stroke, most of their effects were in place, and the boxes nearly emptied of their contents. With some slight preparations the two girls descended the stairs, and entered the room where they had left their aunt.

"Fancy her not coming with us, her own nieces, to show us our rooms," whispered Angela, as they stood together on the threshold.

"Miss Maria had endued herself with a gown richer, more rustling, more be-flounced and more be-furbelowed than the other. She came forward, sounding like the sails of a yacht as the wind flaps them, and drawing her nieces in, said, "Here is your uncle, my dears."

"My dears" were confronted by Mr. Lawless in a scrimped and rusty evening suit. He kissed them each on the cheek, and bade them welcome kindly. To a youth with a crutch he then led them, and Fox held out his hand, with a flush suffusing his usually pale features, and with down-cast eyes.

Angela took the listless hand in one equally listless, and with some faint word of greeting, turned away. But Clemence, grasping his slender, cold fingers strongly, stooped and kissed his cheek, an attention he seemed hardly to know whether to resent or to like. Then dinner was pronounced to be ready, and they went into the dining-room.

" You will find us—ha—simple people, plain people," remarked Mr. Lawless as they took their places. " A little money goes such a little way, such a very little way."

" How thankful I am that we have our own meagre, yet independent income," thought Angela with inward rejoicing. She bowed her head slightly in token of assent, and saw all her day-dreams of the beauty and completeness of an English gentleman's home, giving up the ghost.

They had half-finished soup, when the door was opened, and a young man walked hastily into the room, making his goal Angela's shining head.

" I am sorry not to have been here before to welcome you," he said, in most agreeable accents. " I have been to the station to meet you," he laughed, " but, unfortunately, it was the wrong train. You, it seems, came by the 4.40." He paused, with an air of hesitation, his lips nearly touching Angela's white and blue-veined temple. Finally, they touched it; and, going over to the other sister, he greeted her in the same fashion.

Angela fixed her large and brilliant eyes upon his charming face with a sense of restored glamour. Clemence, too, scanned her cousin with her long, soft eyes, and seemed to find him an agreeable object of contemplation.

Then the new comer subsided into his seat, and hurriedly swallowed his soup, while Mr. Lawless maundered on to everybody in general. " A good passage you say you had ? That was fortunate ; and in March ! They used to have immense placards, ' Beware of Pickpockets,' on the Liverpool Dock ; have they them there still ?"

" Yes," said Clemence, " they have."

" What a sense of insecurity those words give one. Yes ; to discover that one's purse is gone cannot be an agreeable sensation. The tricks of their trade are so numerous, and so ingenious. Wooden hands—ha—a large plaid thrown over the arm ; a saw-knife ; accomplices."

" It is an art, is it not ?" observed Angela, with a smile. " I believe, among each other, they are very proud of being proficients."

" I should be very sorry to have any means of knowing," said Miss Maria, in a strong-minded manner, although the remark had not been addressed especially to her.

" I am quite willing to be told in print, Aunt Maria," returned Angela.

" Are you fond of riding ?" said Bertie,

changing the subject, and speaking to Angela.

" After the fashion of knowing very little about it, and only being willing to ride a very quiet horse, and never going very far, or without having some one close beside me, and never trotting,—yes, I am."

Bertie, who had had full-fledged plans of changing the pair of lean carriage horses for tolerable ones that could be either ridden or driven, now felt the keen edge of his determination to be blunted.

" Clemence is a much braver horsewoman than I am," Angela continued, glancing over at her.

Bertie, being less attracted by the more ordinary features and colouring of the elder sister, expressed little interest in her horsemanship. Anything more exquisite than the white and delicate loveliness of his younger cousin, he thought he had never seen. Angela, for her part, thought that a better-looking man than her cousin Bertie could not exist. For his sake, she reconciled herself to the shrivelled, haggard sexagenarian, her uncle, and the self-engrossed, self-considering, self-cossetting spinster, her aunt; and to the grim and hideous room, and the queer old servants, and the ramshackle waggonette, and the weird and dreamy boy opposite her, who was at that moment devouring her with his eyes.

Yet the barrack-like furniture here, and the shabby furniture of the sitting-room, the plain food, the impoverished fires, filled her with unquenchable amazement. Their father had been in the habit of speaking of his elder brother as a man very well off. What was the meaning of it? Had his money gone the way of all flesh? or— striking thought—was it stuffed up chimneys, in old stocking-legs, or secreted beneath the roots of trees in old preserved-apricot cans?

And this debonnair and thorough-going gentleman, Bertrand, was it not possible for him to right the ricketty and shambling household? In after days, she understood how powerless Bertie was, and how dependent upon his father.

This party of stranger-kindred took the rapid strides towards intimate relations that kin must and will take, according to the natural law of things. Before the two girls had risen from the table, they found themselves in possession of an assured and homelike feeling, a ready habilitation of the manners and customs of Creyke.

Bertie lingered but ten minutes at the table with his father; and, leaving him and Fox having a little altercation together, entered the small sitting-room where his mother's beautiful blue eye looked meltingly at him, and seating himself beside Angela, continued a conversation that her rising from the table had interrupted.

Clemence listened to her aunt's narration (which included pathological details) of an "attack" of a friend of hers, with a patience that left nothing for the narrator to desire.

Angela, looking like a lovely white porcelain transparency, leaned back in a shabby chintz-covered chair, and pretended to follow the intricate windings of a point-lace pattern, while she said pretty things to her cousin Bertrand.

Bertie considered his young relatives gifts of the gods to their dull household, and the thought that they were permanent inmates, and no bright birds of passage, filled him with secret joy.

" How long will it be before you begin to feel yourself at home in this ' Abomination of Desolation ?' " he asked lightly, yet waited eagerly for the reply.

" I begin to feel already as if my tendrils clasped," answered Angela, laughing at her own expression.

" I am delighted," he said earnestly, " delighted. Perhaps you will be at last able to forget the decrepid furniture, the shabby carpets, the general air of miserliness, which—I can own to you—attaches itself to the whole place. You will be good and gracious enough, I hope, not to convict me of aiding and abetting the strange, the unaccountable penuriousness that seems to clutch the old house, and the old land, and ourselves, like the grasping claw of a bird of prey."

" Be sure that I acquit you now, here, this moment," rejoined Angela, with quick-sighted, quickly-apprehending sympathy.

Then, by tacit consent they allowed the subject to fall away from them, nor was it one to be resumed for many, many a long day.

Clemence was heartily pleased when her crippled cousin, followed by his father, entered the room. It was not Mr. Lawless's practice to add himself to the family circle after dinner. He usually secreted himself in a grim justice-room, and burrowed amongst papers in every stage of yellowness and antiquity, and rattling newness. To-night, however, it seemed obligatory for him to spend an hour or so with his newly-arrived nieces; he owed it to their consanguinity, besides, they appeared to him inoffensive and agreeable as young women could well be. He was going to be fond of them, he told himself. He seated himself at the other side of Clemence, while Fox, with eyes that shamed the lynx, watched Angela's shining fair hair, her white straight features and glisten-eyes and teeth. He liked her dress, too, of a tint that Angela affected, and now, in her half-mourning, indeed, she seldom wore any other. A "*gris perle mourant*," she would have told you it was.

"She is like a strip of moonshine," thought the boy; "if she watched a fel-low in his sleep, I believe she would strike him mad, as the moon is sometimes known to do—mad or foolish! I dare not go nearer to her and speak to her, though she is my first cousin. How coldly she took my hand; the other kissed me— a cool, unimaginative kiss. If *she* kissed one, it would be with an unworded thought, or wish, or fancy; there is a fancy be-hind every glance of those blue eyes of hers."

The object of the boy's musing, regarded him not. Once or twice she addressed some gentle word to his father, and then resumed her conversation with Bertie.

And so the evening passed ; novel, yet made familiar by the certainty that it was only the first of many that would follow. They partook of tea ; an unwonted luxury, and one that was doomed not to be continued, for Mr. Lawless's heart ached at every sip ; and it was bad for his nieces' nerves; bad, too, for Fox, who was nervous; bad for his own pocket. Why, it would cost him four shillings a week! and four shillings, he would have told you, was no inconsiderable sum.

"Clemence," said Angela that night to her sister, when they were locked into their room, " it is all so different from what I had imagined, and yet, do you know, I don't mind it! There is something so bizarre, so weird, in the scrimping and grinding of Uncle Francis; he's a sort of miser, don't you think? or else he has lost all his money—but no, it cannot be that from something Bertrand said to me to-night. Oh, Clemence, he is a miser! Imagine having a real miser for one's own uncle! Let us look in impossible places, and see if we shall find a boot with the foot filled with bank-notes ; or an unsuspicious teapot in a suspicious place, filled with sovereigns."

" Now, Angela, are you beginning a new set of fancies ? What did Bertie tell you ?"

" Oh, don't call him Bertie ; call him Bertrand—charming name." Then she repeated her cousin's words.

" There is nothing of the miser about *him*, at all events, that I am sure," said Clemence. " And I really never should think of calling Uncle Francis 'a real miser,' as you say. He is saving, avaricious, penurious, grudging every penny, perhaps. But as for hiding sovereigns, and burying bank-notes, that is nonsense ! *Miser*—why what a word it is ; connected in one's mind with monstrosities."

" Yes," broke in Angela, eagerly, and standing bathed in her silken hair, " filthy creatures, squalid, wretched, and loathsome beyond belief ;—perhaps, one day, Uncle Francis, sliding from bad to worse, may come to be like them. Can't you fancy him dressed in old coal sacks, and eating tallow candle-ends, without shoes and stockings, with finger-nails long, hooked, pointed, and yellow as a condor's?"

"No, no," cried Clemence, genuinely shocked, "do not be fantastic; remember, Angela, he is our father's brother."

"I could wish that 'our father's brother' owned drawers that would open," was all Angela's reply, as she struggled with one of those obstinate receptacles. "Clemence, girl of thews and sinews, help me to pull!" And the young lady like a strip of moon-shine set her teeth hard, and shook the obdurate handles fiercely.

Clemence came immediately to her assistance, and having opened it, returned to her evening devotions, for she numbered amongst her other "commonplace" excellences, a most true and simple piety. Angela, in her gray dressing-gown, presently flung herself down upon her knees, and breathed a short, a very short prayer; and during it, absolute silence reigned.

CHAPTER III.

 MOST untempting morning was their lot, as they saw when they looked out of their window. Clouds, as dark as the embodiment of evil wishes, drifted heavily overhead, sending down occasional violent showers that chilled the air, and soaked the ground, and obscured the waving outline of the distant hills.

Precisely at eight o'clock, they had been waked by a sound on the other side of the wall, mysterious at first, but soon explicable. A sound that made them shiver and gasp sympathetically, and fancy that they heard a strangled wheeze. It was Miss Lawless

taking a shower-bath, which she was cele-
brated for doing with great bravery. Every
morning, with the utmost regularity, their
ears were greeted by the same sound, and
it came to be the signal for Clemence to
spring from her small iron bedstead, and
begin her toilette.

On this, the first day, there was much of
expectancy and anticipation to the two girls.
They stood upon the threshold of a new
and untried life, and, moreover, a life that
was to continue for an unknown length of
time.

Fireless they had gone to bed, and fireless they arose, and with numb fingers
and blue, appeared in the dining-room.
On their way, Angela had clutched her
sister's arm with dramatic fervour, and,
drawing her to a window on the landing,
bade her look out.

" See the reality of my day-dreams," she
whispered; "see the realization of my
dream-pictures, of the home that I was
coming to !" She pointed as she spoke
to ragged hedges, and dilapidated out-

buildings, and a forlorn summer-house, like an overgrown mushroom, which disfigured a spot that in summer was thickly shaded by a fern-leaved beech, and a fine lime.

"Strange! I am not so heartsore about the quashing of my agreeable fancies as I should have judged that I would be."

"I am so glad," answered Clemence, kindly; "indeed, I never saw you bear one of your disenchantments so well."

Then they went on down the creaking staircase.

Miss Maria in a dark magenta serge gown, over which black snaky patterns crawled, interlacing each other, and curling about each other like a reptilian tea-party, was breakfasting according to unvarying regimen. Fox had not yet appeared; Bertie was there, reading the newspaper.

"How I hope the day will turn out fine, after all," he said; "I had hoped that you would be able to drive, walk, or something. Not that there is anything very tempting to be seen—ruins, Carre Abbey—do you like ruins?"

"Never having seen any, we don't possess the proper qualification for judging whether we like them or not," replied Clemence, "but we shall be charmed to see them; shall we not, Angela?"

"Yes, of course," responded Angela, "but, remember, Bertrand, we are not to be made objects of entertainment, as if we were strangers."

"The weather to-day is not going to be fit to do anything in," remarked Miss Maria, as if she were the weather's mouthpiece, or interpreter. "Are you not very cold in that dress, dear?" she continued, in an aggressive tone, turning to Angela, who had on a gray gown, fine and clinging, but thick in texture.

"My dress is very much warmer than it looks," returned Angela, quickly.

"It is too pale for winter," said Miss Lawless, who really was eminently truthful and outspoken. No one had ever heard her deviate one hair's breadth from the bald fact. Certainly, sometimes, there was a kind of grandeur in her unswerving vera-

city, for she forced into the piercing light
of day truths concerning herself that might
quite as easily have been suppressed. All
the slights she had ever endured, all the
great and petty rudenesses that she had ever
been subjected to, all the blunders she had
ever committed, all the malapropos speeches
that she had ever made, she told without
flinching. But if she was hard on herself, she was ten times more unsparing of
others.

" I like these pale and delicate tints,"
Angela continued, in her even tones; " I
am not fond of coarse, strong colours."

" H'm," said Miss Maria, crackling her
newspaper as she took it up from beside
her plate. Then Mr. Lawless entered,
with a frosty tip to his nose, and greeted
his nieces kindly.

"A bad day," he said. "Weather is where
England fails; yet we are not shrivelled
with heat, nor can any one say that it is un-
wholesome to go without a fire in one's
bedroom in the winter. No, no, we are
moderate, if disagreeable. What is the

name of to-day? Ha! Saturday; Adie comes down this evening to spend Sunday; he has not been before for a considerable time. Another cousin for you, yes."

"Adie," repeated Angela; "I am afraid, if he looks at all like you," turning to Bertie, "that I shall not be able to call him by that infantile name."

"He is very much darker, and a good deal taller," said Bertie, laughing; "it is astounding how nursery names cling. I could not call Adie anything but Adie any more than I could call Fox, John. Adrian is such a showy name, too; I could never manage it."

"And is Adrian himself showy?" inquired Angela.

"He is rather good-looking," answered Bertie, and as he spoke, Fox, on his crutch, came slowly into the room. Clemence gave him good-morning in her usual gracious and genial tones; Angela, in her listless and faint ones.

"Do they know no people about here?" she was saying to herself just at that

moment; "have they no neighbours who
are also friends ? Has my handsome cousin no object within riding or walking
distance ?"

As if in answer to her thoughts, Mr.
Lawless said, " Somewhat tame, and same,
your life here will be, my dear children;
the people about honour me with that—ha
—that amount of attention, consideration,
and hospitality which is usually accorded
the poor and unpopular man."

" Hospitality to give, wants hospitality
to get," said Fox, bravely; "yet Bertie
might get on well enough if he chose—
if he was not such a proud file-gnawer."

Both sisters turned a little towards
Bertie, who said nothing. It was a moment
of slight embarrassment; disclosures of a
disagreeable nature are difficult things to
make conversational playthings of.

" Anything will seem gay to us, after St.
Dominic, where we only existed," said
Clemence; "lived, we could not have been
said to do, we had so few friends, so few

amusements, so little that was congenial to us."

" Pray what did you do ?" demanded Fox, looking at Angela.

" We snow-shoed, we skated, we whirled over the roads in a small carriole, drawn by a Canadian pony with a mouth of ada- mant, and a temper of Judas ; once, I froze an ear, by way of variety, and one evening Clemence came home with her chin white as chalk — frozen, of course. We had a few pet cats and dogs, but they quickly went the way of all flesh, were frozen generally. They would run away and get themselves lost, and the next morning, or the one after, would be dis- covered on the door-step, stiff and stark."

" Then your life here will certainly bear to be contrasted with the old one," said Bertie.

" Doubtless," she replied, with a smile and gracious look.

How lovely she was when she smiled, Fox thought ; her lips were not red and full, like her sister's, but they were so curling and flower-like; they reminded him of pale pink geranium petals.

" Have you any commands for Barport," said Bertrand as he rose from the table, " for I am going to ride there presently?"

No, the sisters had no command for Barport.

" Are you going for a ride through that excellent imitation of the deluge?" asked Angela petulantly, " why you will come home Bertie-and-water."

" Weather is nothing to me," he answered, " and I promise not to return in a diluted state."

They went into the sitting-room then; at least, the two girls, Miss Maria, and Fox did so. Mr. Lawless was left to whatever avocations he usually followed in the morning.

Angela, going to the window, watched her cousin mount and ride away. He espied her white and lovely face peeping out, and lifting his hat with a bright smile, walked his horse down the neglected avenue.

" 'Wandering companionless,'" quoted
Angela in a whisper to her sister, as he
vanished from sight; "don't you see
exactly how it all is? He is too proud to
accept hospitality from the people about
here, when his father is qualified in every
respect to return it, yet, from the horrid
blot of miserliness, will not do so."

"He is quite right, I mean Bertie is
quite right," answered Clemence quietly.
"Angela, I wish that you would not lean
your whole weight on me, and buzz
whispers into my ear, like that; come, let
us talk to Aunt Maria."

"Aunt Maria is in act of devotion,"
said Angela.

It was true ; Aunt Maria read the Psalms
for the day, and the lesson, not in the re-
tirement of her own apartment, but before
the public eye, as represented by whoever
happened to be in the room with her.

In her easy-chair, with her large, handsome Church Service in her large, unhand-
some hand, Miss Maria was allowing the
words of Holy Writ to mirror themselves

upon her retina; whether they sank to her inner consciousness or not, forbid that one should judge.

For the servants at Creyke there were no morning prayers. During their performance, if they had had them, Mr. Lawless would have fidgeted himself into a nervous fever. They cost nothing—true; but they never opened the day for those few and hard-worked retainers at Creyke. It was not the way.

The time seemed very long to both girls upon that rainy morning; to Bertie, it passed with a tolerable celerity. Is it not always so? The man, rides away—and forgets. The woman, remains—and remembers.

With the rain gliding off his india-rubber coat, and trickling down his face as it fell from the brim of his hat, he entered the village, or rather small town, of Barport, and making direct for the saddler's shop, dismounted, and holding his horse Elspeth's bridle, cast his eyes about him for a suitable small boy to lead the animal to the

shelter of the inn yard round the corner.
As he flung his leg over her back, and
lightly descended to the ground, he was
aware of a pair of immense, babyish brown
eyes, elevated at about the height of five
feet three inches from the ground, which
were steadily regarding him. It was a
child ; or, half-child, half-woman ; as for
her garments, Bertie could honestly have
declared that they were one great tatter, and
of the nameless écru tint, not of fashion,
but of extreme poverty. The little face,
peeping above the tatterdemalion's shawl,
was pink as a cyclamen ; made to blush
perpetually by the too ardent kisses of the
last summer's sun and wind.

The same sun had bleached the hair
that should have nearly approached black,
to a rich, mahogany brown, and the locks,
curling in the moist air, shaded a forehead
infantile and guileless as that of a cherub.

Bertie noted the quaint, the indescribable, the piteous and squalid prettiness of
face and form, and muttered, half to himself, half to the child, who had not ceased

to regard him with a fixed, marmoset's stare: "Strange! a fellow never can see a boy when he happens to want one."

"Please, sir, d'ye want your horse held?" this, in a rustic's voice, untinctured by the slightest rustic shyness, from her of the rags.

"I do want my horse held, certainly," said Bertie with a smile, "or rather, I want her taken round to the 'Bugle' yard."

"I'll take he," cried the child with alacrity, "gi'e me hold." She laid four gipsy fingers on Elspeth's bridle as she spoke, beside Bertie's soaked, dog-skin covered ones.

"Not so fast!" he cried, trying to shake them off, while Elspeth expanded her nostrils, and snuffed, and snorted, over the torn brown straw hat that almost touched her velvet muzzle. "Not so fast; girls are not supposed to do this kind of thing; run round the corner, and see if you cannot see a boy."

The child shook her head.

"Gi'e it to me," she cried again, with a

broad smile; "I'll take him every bit as good as a boy could do, and bring him again when you whistles for I."

"Ain't you afraid of horses?" asked Bertie, looking at the little reed, with her mignonne and delightful face.

"No."

Bertie still clung to the bridle that the four childish fingers had not for an instant relaxed their hold of. The rain poured in torrents, the gutters were running rivers; there was not one human creature visible; no one sallied from the saddler's shop to his assistance; finally he relinquished the rein, and entered the shop; yet he could not refrain from watching the slight young figure, and the hand that was laid caressingly on Elspeth's black neck.

"I must give her a shilling; by George I will! A girl to hold my horse!" Then turning to James, the saddler, who had also heard the foregoing remark, he entered upon the transaction for which he had come. He concluded it, running in debt for a lady's saddle with all the sans souci in the world, and going to the door, gave a shrill whistle.

The rain for the moment had ceased, and black, jagged, low-lying clouds racked swiftly overhead. In three minutes he heard the sharp clatter of his horse's hoofs, and Elspeth and her attendant came quickly round the corner; the child keeping up to the horse's trot, with flying feet.

"You have both been quite sheltered from the rain?" inquired Bertie, looking into the child's large, hazel eyes.

She nodded.

" He's a pretty fellow," she volunteered, touching Elspeth's shoulder with a reverential admiration.

"Would you like to know her name?" asked Bertie with his engaging smile. The child nodded again.

" Elspeth," said Bertie.

She repeated the word after him twice or thrice, and clung still to the creature, relinquishing the bridle, but clutching the mane that was tossing in the wind, as though loath to let her go.

" Have you ever seen me before ?" asked Bertie, waxing a bit inquisitive, although the child was but one of the shreds of humanity, for whom circumstance seems to have as little mercy as has the wind for a broken straw.

" Plenty o' times," returned the child without hesitation, "plenty, plenty."

" And do you like horses very much ?"

" I do. One o' these days I'll ride 'em."

Bertie laughed, and tossed her a shilling, not caring to prolong the conversation, and discover the germ of inborn proclivity, of which this roughly-expressed intention and desire were the upspring. He was not one to probe into the occult, as regards humanity; he was a careless young man who mentally touched one degree above mediocrity, that was all.

The girl seemed considerably amazed at a douceur so beyond her expectations, or indeed her desert. But the look of astonishment was quickly succeeded by one of delight, as she threw the shilling into the air, and caught it in her brown hand.

Then Bertie mounted, and she regarded him, so doing, with unmixed admiration.

" What is your name ?" he said, amused by the look, and lingering.

" Elspeth," replied the child with a grin.

" Nonsense—is it ?"

" Noa."

" Then why did you tell me such a fib ?"

" 'Cause I likes the name."

" But I didn't ask you what you liked, I asked you your name."

The child began to fondle the horse, which received the attention with indifference, as it was a stranger's hand.

" Elspeth," she repeated as if to herself.

" Good-bye, I must go home.—My name's Doll."—This suddenly over her shoulder, as she scudded away.

He watched her run down a lane, that led he knew to the mill, and to a certain grimy cottage which stood close by the osiers that grew on the verge of the mill-stream. Often he had fished in that same stream above the mill, and slaked his thirst in it lower down, where it rushed noisily between its confines, shaded by the trembling willow branches.

He watched her until she was out of sight, and then took his homeward road, going at a smart pace that he might be in time for luncheon.

There never were girls so winning, so companionable, so amusing as his two cousins, Bertie thought, as, having tested them during that entire long, wet afternoon, he had now come to his room to dress. Never were there dearer, sweeter young women; as for Angela, she was fascination itself. What a magnolia white skin, what large and bright blue eyes, what glittering teeth. And could any one in the world have such sweet ways about them as Clemence had? Such tender and sympathetic tones of voice. "Adie!"—he exclaimed aloud, as the thud of a portmanteau in a neighbouring room snapped the thread of his reflections—"he said he should be in time for dinner."

He ran down to greet his brother, and accompanied him to his room while he made his preparations for dinner. He struck into the subject of the cousins, without loss of time.

"They are such capital girls, Adie," he said ; "and excessively good looking, especially the younger, Angela ; though Clemence is very handsome ; in a ball-room she would probably be the more striking of the two. We are all delighted with them ; governor, Aunt Maria, and all. They are fresh to everything, but not rustics ; they are amusing, but not slangy ; full of 'go,' but not fast. The governor is pleased with them because they seem to expect nothing, or want nothing but what they have ; there has been no change made, as you have probably seen for yourself already. Aunt Maria likes them because they are evidently going to allow her to assume the dictatorial with them ; Fox likes them because they are new, have sweet voices, and are good to look at."

"And you ?" asked his brother carelessly.

"I ? I like them because they are jolly girls, and cousins, of course."

Adrian, who at that instant was regarding his own dark visage in the glass, turned, and looked at his brother's bright and symmetrical one.

"I'm ready to go down," he said, abruptly, and turning, marched out of the room and downstairs.

There was no one in the drawing-room when they entered it, but presently the rustle of a woman's garments was heard on the stairs, and Angela, by herself, made her appearance.

She saw the spirited profile of her new cousin, defined against the faded amber window-curtains; dark, bold, full of energy and fire. He turned, and she extended her small, pale hand, which he grasped in his own, saying (for Bertie had not thought of going through with any such formality as mentioning their names to one another),

"You are Angela?"

"And you," replied Angela with an answering smile, "are Adrian?"

She looked especially lovely that evening, although she was all in black, save for a ruffle of tulle round her neck; so high that it touched the lobes of her little waxen ears.

It was not five minutes before Clemence appeared; fresh, red-lipped, radiant, with drops of cold water sparkling like diamonds among her dark hair where it grew upon the temples. She greeted her cousin warmly and with an agreeable air of having had a previous acquaintance with him— perhaps not in this life—but in a state of pre-existence. Then Miss Maria appeared, and Mr. Lawless; and Fox straggled in with evidences of much brain-work, and no fresh air, upon his spare and delicate countenance, and then they all went into the dining-room.

"And how is town, Adie?" inquired Mr. Lawless, frowning a little, as he examined his long filbert nails, with the air of a connoisseur.

"The city," said Adie, a shade bitterly, "is as rich in mud and smoke, and as destitute of light, and air, and sunshine as it usually is at the end of March."

"Spring is coming—ha—and the London season, and taxes to the Londoners, and spring lamb and asparagus for those who can afford to buy 'em; and the poor-rates; and Lady Day will soon be here. So runs time away."

"Father," said Bertie, with the decision of tone that springs not from a sudden impulse, but from a well-considered determination, "I should like to sell those abominable screws of ours, and, by adding a moderate sum, get a pair of horses that shall be neither gone in the fore-legs, nor in the enjoyment of a bone-spavin, as the two pretty creatures in the stable are."

Mr. Lawless exhibited a painful medium between extreme irritation with his son for the evil suggestion and determination not to infringe the decencies and betray his vexation.

"Another time, another time," he said, waving his hand, "we will talk about it; the maladies of the horse are not agreeable subjects for dinner-table discussion. I do not know that I care to part with the—ha

—the carriage horses; they seem to me passable enough nags. Keep what you've got, and get what you can," he added, suddenly turning to Clemence, with a slight grimace and smile, "*if* you can; if you can't, be the object of your own sincerest compassion."

" The idea might be dressed up to sound attractive," said Angela, listlessly; " or a sort of verbal rose-velvet mask, you know, trimmed with point lace, and the idea under it."

" Very well; dress it, or mask it, and present it to us,"· he answered, darting an approving look at her.

" Faith ! I am not half quick enough, or clever enough," she replied, laughing.

" Enjoy what you've got, and give what you can, would sound more attractive to many people," said Clemence.

" It is the duty of everybody to live well within their income, and not think too much of enjoyment," observed Miss Maria, looking up, and joining in the conversation. "*Well* within it," she repeated; "and I should feel that I was not doing my duty towards myself—indeed, that I was doing myself great injustice to give in anything but the smallest sums."

Miss Maria often gave the broadest generalities the closest personal application, which was both embarrassing and irritating.

" Oh, of course!" returned Clemence, in confusion ; " oh dear, yes! I had no idea of meaning—of thinking——"

" I must rescue my floundering relative," thought Angela. " And it is so odious to do one's self injustice, is it not ?" she said, looking at her aunt; " it is like striking one's own dear head a resounding thump against something, or stepping up a step which does not exist, or going to a dinner-party the day before, or being the first person at a ball, or treasuring up a retaliative speech to say to some one we hate and then forgetting it when we do see them; there is no one to blame but ourselves——"

Miss Maria cut her short; she was swelling with offence ; claptrappy, frivolous, girlish chatter she detested ardently, and she summoned her hardest tones, and her most dog-fishy glances, as she replied,

"You talk so low and so fast, my dear, that I have only been able to catch a word here and there; but I think that before *servants* one should be careful of what one says."

"Servants—careful!" repeated Angela, elevating her eyebrows, and drawing down the corners of her sensitive mouth.

"Poor old Stainer," cried Fox, bursting out laughing, "would be pleased, Aunt Maria, if he could know that you gave him credit for walking off with a tray, and understanding a foreign tongue at the same time."

"Angela is very fanciful," said Clemence to her aunt, half apologetically.

"So I should judge," rejoined Miss Maria, in metallic tones.

"Yes, I am," remarked Angela, for herself. "Let me write you a fairy tale, and come in and read you to sleep with it; you know you were complaining this morning of lying awake so long after you went to bed."

" Thank you," responded Miss Maria, not ill-naturedly, " I won't trouble you. I was brought up by my grandmother," she continued, after a moment's pause; " I was thought very well, and properly educated, and brought up; but no doubt my ideas are old-fashioned."

" If they are our great-grandmothers', I suppose they would hardly be called advanced now," returned Angela, impertinently; and no one in the room liked her better for that impertinence. To Bertie it seemed an unpleasant glimpse of the real woman hidden away behind the sweet girl's face, and sheltered by the sweet girl's manner.

Miss Maria made no retort; but she turned very purple, and the veins in her temples throbbed. Before long, she had forgotten the slight to her grandmother, though, and was eating her dinner with her usual mixture of fear and joy.

CHAPTER IV.

OROTHY, or Doll, went flutter-
ing along through the rain, sundry scraps and ends of raiment
flapping damply against her ankles as she
ran. It was not far to that combination of
dog-kennel, hen-house, and human habita-
tion which she called "home." Ah! indeed,
it was " ever so humble;" and it was addi-
tionally ever so dirty, and ever so damp,
and ever so poverty stricken! Being the
"sole daughter" of her father's "house and
heart," there were no Dolls, male and female, smaller than herself to share her
scrimped and forlorn existence.

Her father, a labourer, did not come

home to a midday meal, and so Doll, who
was to-day somewhat late, dined at a shelf
in the cupboard, without going through the
ceremony of placing her cold bacon and
potatoes on the table.

Having satisfied her hunger, she went
back to where she had laid her shilling ;
and regarding it with a loving eye (for it
represented to her food and amusement),
picked it up, and went out into a disorderly
back yard, where she dipped a battered tin
saucepan into the hogshead full of rain-
water, and scrubbed the precious piece with
soft-soap and a small tatter (torn from her
own personal apparel for the purpose), until
it shone white and clean.   One or two ab-
ject hens, with feathers that were feathers
in naught but the name, came and stood
drearily on one leg and watched her.   She
darted into the house, and returning with
scraps of potatoes in her wet hands, flung
them to them ; and they squabbled, and
scratched, and clucked over them, and forgot their wet misery.

As she was throwing the soapy water

away, a labourer's heavy, unelastic thump
of a step sounded in the kitchen inside, and
Doll knew that her father had returned
from his day's work a mile away.

There were no greetings exchanged between them; amenities seem to die, suffo-
cated in the atmosphere of extreme poverty,
fragile exotics that they are, shedding perfume and brightness over life, blending a
slight, bright woof, with the dull warp of
daily worries, vexations, and cares. Alas!
the poor, amongst the " shards and thorns
of existence," have them not.

None of the small, pleasant, gilded de-
ceits that smooth and sweeten that smoother
and sweeter life of which they know nothing, are theirs. The truths of life they
have; and they are always to them hard,
rough, and ugly.

John Drake had at his heels the dog who
habitually guarded the tin-pail containing
his master's bacon and potatoes—his dinner, in fact—a nondescript animal, with a
canine cark and care written upon his
ragged and wobegone countenance. In

his brown eyes was the fidelity, the unswerving loyalty that nothing could shake.
The kicks and blows that would long ago
have alienated a fellow human being from
surly John Drake, seemed only to attach
him the more firmly.

It was one of Doll's life-efforts to win the
same devotion from Jack that her father
gained; but she failed. All her entice-
ments of scraps for his hungry maw, caresses for his rough, much pommelled head,
were in vain. Jack was John's to kick, to
abuse, to kill if need be.

Doll ran into the kitchen, tossing her
shilling in the air as she went, and catching
it, making no comment to her father regarding it; she knew that it would not be
necessary.

"Wot yer got there?" quoth honest John,
grasping her arm with one hand, while with
the other he deprived her fingers of their
prize.

"What's the good of my telling yer,"
answered Doll, "if yer bound to see for
yourself?"

" Where did it come from ?"

" It come from a gentleman's pocket,
where it had been alonger his handker-
cher."

" Well, and how did it get out a his
pocket and into yourn ?"

" I ain't got a pocket!" observed Doll,
with a laugh.

He shook her, to let her know that an
answer must be given without delay; and
she spoke at once, and rapidly,

" I held his horse for him ; I held it for
more'n ten minutes; when I come out, he
gi' it to me."

John, with the grudge of a magpie that
is being robbed of its " loot," restored the
shilling to his child, and bade her set the
kettle on the fire (for there was a small
fire in the little stove).

Doll obeyed, and seating herself upon
the cindery hearth, dried her ragged self as
best she could.   John Drake, who was also
well drenched, took off his coat, kicked off
his hob-nailed, mud-encrusted shoes, and
waited with impatience for the kettle to boil

" Happen the gentleman was one o' Squire Lawless's sons?" he said, interrogatively, after a long pause.

Doll nodded, but somewhat doubtfully, and watched a look, darker than the lowering clouds outside, creep over her father's face; for Mr. Lawless was John's landlord, and not loved by John, who had found him a man of flint.

"The young 'un is no liker his feyther than is——" John paused; his mental resources not being great enough to produce, an illustration at a moment's notice.

" Than is a rat to a horse," supplied Doll, taking the kettle off. " Kittle's bilin', feyther," she added, and proceeded thereupon to make tea. She helped her father to consume it, and also sundry fat, thick rashers of the inevitable bacon, and thicker slices of brown bread. After her father had stuffed his clay pipe with tobacco, and begun his evening refreshment and solace, she tumbled the cups, and spoons, and plates into a wooden bowl of hot water, and running gaily out of the house, left them to soak.

The rain was over and gone; the evening sky was crowded with clouds of varie-
gated, stormy hues—lurid and russet, and
dun, and livid, and lead-coloured, and here
and there faint primrose as some jagged
corner caught a stray ray of sunshine.

Doll went nimbly down to the mill-
stream, which was near enough for her to
hear it at night, even with the window
shut, and stood looking at the little brawling strip of water that had such a clear and
treble voice out under the open sky, and in
the free air, and such a perturbed and
hollow gurgle as it rushed between the
stone walls that fettered it here, and under
the dark and solid archway, from which
issued, even in the hottest days, a cool,
damp smell that Doll loved.

She had brought out with her a thick
slice of bread, scalloped with bites; and,
notwithstanding that it was winterish, and
she was cold, stood, according to habit,
munching and staring down into the
limpid water.

As she finished the last remaining scrap

of crust, she ran in again and began her hated task of taking the dishes from their bowl, and drying them on a towel that had grown threadbare in the service.

Then Doll's housewifery was over for the day. Her father needed none of her service in mixing and draining the small glass of gin and water upon which he usually retired. It was the signal for Doll to take herself off—the trickling of the strong white liquid into their one cracked glass—and, jumping to her feet, she gave a good-night nod to her father, and flew up the crazy stairs, which were little better than a ladder, to her small sleeping place, an ugly loft enough, with its flock-bed, and tattered print quilt, and one unsafe chair.

Doll possessed an India-rubber comb, with half the teeth gone; and once, a very long time ago, so long that she had almost outlived the memory of it, she had owned a brush : it had vanished in some untoward manner, she forgot now what the manner had been. The comb was a patriarch, and served but poorly to disentangle the tresses of Doll's tri-coloured hair. For Doll's abundant locks were, by turns, deep brown, pale brown, and, at the ends, were bleached to what nearly approached gold.

The one chair was useless, as to its legitimate purpose, for on it stood a coarse china basin, and a dented pewter ewer, which were the just causes of Doll usually having an average clean face and hands.

Doll delighted in going to bed—the delight of a young beast of the field that perishes. To-night, she was not long in kicking off her rain-stiffened shoes, in divesting herself of her still damp rags, and seeking and finding " sweet repose " upon the flockbed, and beneath the quilt, through whose gaps and rents the stuffing was oozing.

As she closed her eyes, she heard the familiar voice of the mill-stream, brawling at, and complaining of, its fetters. In summer, when the little casement was thrown open, she could hear the osiers murmuring and sighing, and whispering laments to one another—not now—this was the deaf and dumb time of the year,

and Doll liked it but little. No wonder
that summer was her favourite season,
it always is the favourite season of the
poor.

CHAPTER V.

NATURE dried her tears, gave smiles of sunshine, and most balmy breaths of wild west wind the following morning, which was a Sunday, and led to the putting on of new gloves, and pretty little bonnets, and a search for little violet Prayer-books on the part of the sisters.

They walked down the terrace steps, across the not too well kept lawn, and through the wild and uneven park, to the small gray church, with its ancient flint-stone tower, and deep, shady porch. They felt some curiosity to see the vicar, for they knew that in a day or two his wife would call. They entered the large pew—a good deal stared at by what congregation there was—behind their Aunt Maria, and followed by Bertie and Adrian. Then Adrian closed the pew-door, and the sisters sank upon their knees, and hid their faces on their little purple Prayer-books.

When they lifted up their heads, the curate had entered the reading-desk ; and him they found to be a placid and pretty young man, about whom it was impossible to harbour anything even as mild as a conjecture. When Mr. North took his place in the pulpit, a sensation took the place of the calm, half-apathy with which they had regarded, and listened to, Mr. Burnaby.

Mr. North was a tall, spare man of fifty, with a fine, almost perfect, head, and pale, noble features. He wore spectacles, but Clemence thought that he owed to them a more complete air of erudition. His voice was deep and clear, yet with the occasional uncertain thrill of a man of very deep feeling.

As he commenced his sermon with a

quotation from Socrates, Angela felt sure
that he was removed from that thing she
detested—the commonplace—and conse-
quently was prepossessed in his favour.

It was a service, neither fantastically
high, nor deadly low—a juste milieu—
which satisfied Angela, who was advanced
in her ideas of how the liturgy should be
conducted, yet did not offend Aunt Maria,
who was ultra low-church.

Clemence had hoped that they might
have an opportunity of exchanging a few
words with Mr. North, but he was not
visible, nor was Mrs. North, his wife, in
church. She was not in strong health,
Bertie told them.

The cousins walked down the gravelled
path between tomb-stones, recording the
(in many instances) surprising names, and
the best qualities of those who lay beneath.

A low phaeton lined with shabby green
awaited Miss Lawless at the gate, and the
girls having both pronounced their pre-
ference for walking home, Miss Lawless

was driven off by old John, with the reins sawing past her fine bonnet, with her flacon, and her gossamer handkerchief, and her handsome Church-service on her lap.

The cousins walked slowly up the hilly road, and presently entered the park. It was warm and pleasant enough to tempt them to linger under the close-growing old trees, and to hunt for the wild violets which were beginning to spring up and hide themselves with their usual modesty. Angela walked delicately by Bertie's side, her fair head a little drooped towards him, while the active tenant of that fair head spun a cobweb of fancies to catch itself in hereafter, suicidally.

Adrian not being satisfied with the undivided companionship of his elder cousin, hurried her along, until at last they found themselves abreast of Bertie and Angela, and listeners to the concluding words of a few very sweet lines that Angela was taking the opportunity to quote to her cousin.

" I am glad that you were not an instant earlier," she said with a glance at her sister, half-malicious, half self-complacent. "Clemence has not patience to hear me quote gems of genius. Now, really Clemence, I do not believe that you could quote two lines of poetry, to save yourself from instant execution, could you ?"

" Indeed, yes," replied the other with that delightful manner of hers, that was so far removed from whimsicality, and yet so buoyantly light-hearted, " I can quote a distich famously, Angela, that shall be exactly appropriate to you :—

" There was a little girl,
    And she had a little curl
    That hung in the middle of her forehead,
And when she was nice, she was very, very nice,
And when she was *not*, she was *horrid*."

Bertie laughed, Angela shrugged her shoulders with a scornful " Is that original ?"

But Bertie said, " Come, let us have another."

" Are you equal to another of the same calibre ?" inquired Angela with an airy contempt for her senior, to which Clemence, fortunately, was hardened.

" Of course I am," answered Clemence promptly, and looking at her sister with a little laugh :

> " Billy Bolaine, he jumped out of bed,
>   He flew at his sister and cut off her head,
>   Which caused his mother a great deal of pain,
>   Let us hope that dear Billy won't do it again."

" What marvellously different young women !" thought Bertie, remembering Angela's

> " The flower that smiles to-day
>   To-morrow dies ;
>   All that we wish to stay,
>   Tempts and then flies," &c.

As for Adrian, his younger cousin seemed to him a curious study. There was a sort of self-admiration about her, not demonstrated by word or act, yet perceptible to him, nevertheless.

Just now she seemed to be allowing Bertie to share that self-admiration, for she was gazing up at him with an odd blending of consciousness of self, and approval of *him.* She remembered to keep her face at the becoming angle, and yet she studied his carefully.

" Love to give, finds ever love to get," says the translator, yet one cannot help but doubt him. What a wise provision of Nature it would seem, were it really the case; yet how it would rob individual histories of the melancholy charm and pity-suffused interest with which they are now invested.

Angela persistently addressed herself to Bertie; not conscious that he was far from showing the same absorption in her, that she did in him; but she had always contrived to weave a kind of spell about the few men with whom she had been thrown. And the introspective view she took of herself was altogether flattering.

" Has the vicar sons and daughters ?" she said.

" He has one son ; no daughters."

" Ah, a fortunate man not to be obliged to add to a supply that exceeds the demand, to swell an unwanted majority. It is not nice to be a drug in the market, and a coal at Newcastle, is it?" she demanded.

"Individually, I don't think you are likely to be made to feel like a Newcastle coal, Angela," he answered.

Angela was pleased, and showed it. Then he went on.

"Henry North is a capital fellow; he is in the——"

"Oh, a soldier," said Angela parenthetically. "I don't want to hear about him," she added, "unless it is something in connection with yourself. Were you boy friends together? Did you rob bird's nests, torture cats, stick pins through butterflies, tie tin cans to the tails of outcast dogs, steal cherries, and tumble off coach-house roofs together?"

"Is that your idea of boy friendships?" asked Bertie laughing.

"It is my idea, yes; not based on any personal observation, please remember. I have known nothing in all my life of boys or their friendships, but I always think this of them : mischief, thy name is boy. But you have not answered me, was this Henry North a friend of your childhood ?"

" Yes, he was," replied Bertie ; " he was very near my own age, and we were great allies as boys, but we never practised the enormities you have catalogued."

" No, I am sure you would not torture a cat, even in the pitiless days of childhood," said Angela.

" Nor would North as a boy have tortured anything that lived," rejoined Bertie.

" Oh !" observed Angela vaguely, not feeling much interest in Henry North, or Henry North's good points.

" Were you more pitiless as a child than you are now ?" inquired Adrian, joining in the conversation, and showing that he had been an attentive listener to what had gone before.

" Ask Clemence," said Angela carelessly, and stooping down to pluck a wild hyacinth that she immediately gave to Bertie.

"*Was* she?" he asked obediently, turning to the older sister.

"She was very cruel to her dolls," said Clemence, "and I think I remember a terrible offence of giving a cat a bit of meat tied to the end of a shoe-string, that she once committed at a tender age. Yes, I think she was more cruel as a child. Why?"

"I—I don't know," answered Adrian at a loss, and using those limp and flabby words, that so often sound the flattest in the language. Then he rallied; "and she has never substituted men of dust, for puppets of sawdust?"

"She has never had an opportunity," said Clemence calmly.

Angela pouted. "We did not know a great many people in St. Dominic, for there were not many to know. There was a regiment stationed there for a short time on account of Fenian disturbances, Angela was about sixteen and a half then; and I have a dreamy recollection of a scarlet face that used to grow redder when it saw her, and a hat with a 'puggry' that was taken off with a flourish when it met her.   I suppose they belonged to a man."

" How hypocritical you are, Clemence, to pretend you don't remember Frank Osgood !"

" You remember him very well, it seems," said Adrian.

"Of course I do : he brought me any number of typical lilies and cherries.   His face was the colour of pink may, all over. He made a laugh do duty for a speech, whenever it was possible; he had a lemon-coloured moustache and saffron hair, and eyes as blue — no, almost as blue as Bertie's."

" *Are* Bertie's eyes blue ?" said Adrian with a fraternal carelessness; " I thought they were gray."

" Irish gray; and Irish gray always means blue."

" That is something like ' auburn ' being pretty-polite for red hair," said Adrian.

" Or like ' tip-tilted like a flower,' being

the poetical equivalent for a turned-up nose," subjoined Clemence.

"I hate eyes so dark that the pupil is indistinguishable," said Angela.

Adrian, whose eyes were as dark as they could well be, smiled grimly at this artless speech of his cousin. But as he considered that he did not in the least wish to establish a claim upon her interest, it did not matter to him. By this time they had reached the house, and the sisters went upstairs to take off their little black bonnets.

"Amuse me this whole, long afternoon," said Angela, coming up to Bertie with a smile, soon after luncheon, as, with Adrian, he stood smoking at a side-door that gave upon the terrace. It was open now, and a brother ornamented either side.

"How am I to set to work?" he inquired; "show you picture-books——"

"Tell me a ghost story," she interrupted imperatively; "a long, dree, ghost story; if it is about our own family, and this house, so much the better; I should like to feel that I am living in a house which owns a

tenant whom the servants only dare speak
of in whispers, and who is only known by
sighs, and rustlings, and mysterious tap-
pings."

Bertie shook his head ; " I fear it is not
one of the Lawless possessions," he said.

" No ? Then one of us should make a
grim tradition for the family ; turn into the
family ghost for the benefit of future
generations. Now, Bertie," she cried with
her faint laugh, and striking her hands together, " don't you think that I have origi-
nated an idea ? If you want to have your
memory treasured, turn into the family
spectre. Don't be the Bertrand who was
mediocre, and is only a name ; an essentially
human creature, who went down into the
dust leaving no story behind him, but be
the ghostly Bertrand, who had some un-
imaginable woe, or committed some unknown crime, and whose perturbed spirit
declines to altogether abandon the old
haunts known to it while in the flesh, and
obligingly turns itself into the family phan-
tom.

" Oh, charming, to be—not Angela the commonplace, who married in the commonplace way—and there is her portrait ; oh, yes ; light hair, not too good looking—that was Angela. Not to be that, but to be the lovely Angela (female phantoms are invariably lovely) who drooped like a frost-nipped flower, and ' grew white as the pearl that was hung at her ear.' Cause, mysterious. Who, beginning by being a trifle weird, went on growing weirder and weirder, until at last in some romantic manner she died, and was considered weird enough, and romantic enough, and unhappy enough to be handed down to posterity as the blood - chilling thing, whose mysterious sounds are heard at midnight, and whose silken skirts rustle for the benefit of timid maidservants, and sceptical guests."

" Come into the morning-room—there is no one there—and I will tell you a ghost story," said Adrian smiling.

They closed the door with alacrity, and all trooped into the deserted morning-room, and taking possession of the chair farthest from Angela, Adrian began abruptly.

"A bishop was once staying in a house——"

"Come," interrupted Bertie, "that is an awfully unartistic beginning—where should a bishop stay?"

"In a house," proceeded Adrian, not heeding; "he slept in a room which was 'grand,' and also 'gloomy and peculiar.' He saw the grandeur at once, but the gloominess and the peculiarity he was not made aware of, until exactly a quarter-past twelve o'clock. Then——"

"Then what?" asked Angela impatiently as he paused.

"Then he was waked by what seemed to him a stealthy footstep, and the jangle of metal. Calling his own active imagination every manner of hard name, the bishop lighted the candle beside his bed, and saw what caused him to cease vituperating his own fancy, and made him grow chilly with terror. A tall young gentleman stood before the dressing-table, with his face carefully turned away from the glass, and also from him, while with a restless hand he fumbled amongst the brushes and combs, and little dressing-case boxes, belonging to the bishop.

" The young gentleman was faultlessly attired in a radiant dress of two centuries ago. His peach-blossom coloured stockings, and high-heeled shoes with diamond buckles, were unexceptionable; so were his claret-coloured coat, and white watered silk waistcoat. In a word, two centuries ago, he would have been thought no end of a swell.

" His hair was powdered as white as snow. 'What do you want, my good sir?' said the bishop, sitting up, and speaking with a dry, and half-paralyzed tongue.

" The young man turned, and with one hand upon his rapier-hilt, advanced with matchless ease and grace; the diamonds on his instep twinkling like glow-worms, as he moved.

" 'This!' he said, striking his face. Then the bishop saw that his eyes were

large, and dark, and that but for one blemish,
he would have been eminently handsome.
Being noseless, is of course a blemish, a
drawback to symmetry, a bar to comeliness; and he had no nose. Apparently it
had been slashed off.

" ' This !' he repeated ; ' I cannot rest
in my coffin without it. Look !' he went
on, coming close beside the bishop's bed,
whose hangings shook, so excessively
did he tremble with dismay. ' Look !'—
and he drew from among the Spanish
lace frills on his breast, an old-fashioned
miniature, in an open gold frame. ' Here
am I, before that hound (may he feel
the grave-worms gnawing him !) mutilated
me. And here'—turning it over—' is
she, who, but for my loss, would have
mouldered by my side. (May she be conscious of the disintegration of her own false
heart : may she feel it to be nourishing
some rank growth of nettles that only a
half-starved ass shall eat !')

" The bishop mechanically turned his
eyes from the maimed face of his grisly

visitor, to the painted one of a girl, very young and fair, with twin-blue devils for eyes, and a particularly mocking and wicked smile. The artist had represented her in the dishevelled style of the period, and if Art had done its work faithfully in depicting her, Nature had not been less faithful.

" 'We drew swords for her, and as his keen blade slashed across my face, the flame of my life's hope went out. He maimed me, and marred me ; he made my beauty to consume away ; he laughed as he did it (may all the dogs of hell claim him as brother !) He looked into my mutilated and bleeding face, and laughed.

" ' " When you have *it* again, you shall have her," ' he fleered.

" ' Then darkness closed in on me. She shrieked out, when she first saw me ; she drew her gold curls over her eyes, and held them there with her white fingers to shut out the horrid sight of my changed face. She said with a shudder, " This is not Ranicar Hungerford ! — I cannot——go, go !" '

" 'So I lost my beauty and *her*. I look for it through the long hours of each night; I shall be looking for it when you are palsied and old; I shall be looking for it when you are laid cold and low.'

" He covered the greater part of his face with his white and jewelled hand, and with his thrilling dark eyes glancing eagerly over the diamonds, he took a searcher's zig-zag course through the room and vanished."

"Very good," said Angela listlessly, as he ceased to speak. " Is it true ?"

" To the foot of the letter."

" Ah, then it is only not bad ; I thought you had invented it on the spur of the moment."

" I believe I could invent one that would make the very down on your cheek stand on end," replied Adrian, in a somewhat miffed tone.

" Oh, Bertie !" said Angela, not paying much attention to him, " can't you really think of one ?"

" Yes," answered he, " I've thought of

one ; you'll find it abominably bad, and it is
literally true, but I'll tell it.

"After I had left Cambridge, the governor munificently allowed me to take three
hundred pounds and frisk over to the
Continent with it.   As it happened, my
great ally at that time was an artist of more
than semi-Bohemian tendencies ; he proposed himself as my companion, and moreover suggested Germany, and the Black
Forest, as a gîte.   I agreed.   At Paris we
added to ourselves a couple of thorough-
going Bohemians ; an actor, Léonce, and
a scribbler, Caillard.   I shall not tell
anything of our journey until we arrived
at a tiny village in the valley of the Alb ;
a little place hiding itself among the dark
pines, and at the hour at which we arrived
(about eight o'clock) very solemn and
gloomy.

"Over our wine, after dinner—or supper
—we were joined by a couple of vagrant uni-
versity students, with the prescribed scar
across the cheek, or on the lip.   They were
of the usual type ; talking a fellow down,

striking a fellow on the shoulder, or thumping the table with their fists to give additional force to what they said ; winding their booted legs round the legs of their chairs, and leaning forward with their elbows on the table and looking at a fellow through their spectacles with their faces an inch from one's own, as they growled out their gutturals.

" They were ferociously in earnest over the story (which they both tried to tell together) of a dilapidated old house, standing with a green ditch round it, that we remembered to have passed as we came along. It was haunted, of course ; and by such an extra-gruesome ghost, that those who lived to tell the tale of a night passed within the walls of its special haunt, told it in the incoherent words of madness. These violent vagrants told the tale with relish, but they admitted *more Germanico*, that they dared not spend a night *alone* within the room that was afflicted by the spectre.

" 'I will sit up there this night, alone,'

said Léonce, the actor, briskly. The students exchanged glances of admiration at this prowess.

" ' Himmel! Will you ?'

" ' Mon Dieu, yes.'

" ' But what are we to do ?' inquired my friend Ruthven.

" ' Stay here, in this room, and wait for me.'

" Getting permission, and the key of the forsaken house, was a prolonged operation. So lengthy, that it was half-past twelve before we watched our hero unlock the door for himself, by the light of the good lantern which he carried ; and with an easy face, and wave of the hand, vanish, closing the door with a clang after him.

" We waited until we saw his light shine out from the window of the room that had been designated to him as the right one, and then returned to the inn. We did not keep ourselves awake with our brilliant conversation. For in all sorts of cramped and uneasy positions we dozed. I must except from an uneasy position the elder of the students, who coiled himself on the floor, and covering himself with a convenient tablecloth to invisibility, seemed to give himself to real repose, while his Wallachian dog crouched beside him.

"And now, Angela, I shall tell you what Léonce did as if I were with him; you don't care for exactitude, you know.

"With his lantern throwing a clear and broad stream of light in front of him, he made his way upstairs, found the haunted room without any difficulty, and entering, placed the lantern so that its shaft of light should strike the open door, and lighting a cheroot, took a libretto from his pocket, and scanned his part in a play of which he was to be star upon his return to Paris.

"It was perfectly still, but for the murmur of the tall pines, as the night wind swept over them. He waited with a contemptuous patience. Not in vain; for the spectre was courteous enough to keep him in suspense but a little while.

"A few sighs, a moan or two, a few rustlings of ghostly garments in the corridor outside, and an apparition was visible in the open doorway, its mouldy wrappings looming white against the blank darkness of the long, unlighted corridor.

"It stood motionless, grinding its teeth. Its eyelids were red as blood, its eyebrows white; the lower part of its face was hidden.

"Léonce's heart gave one great bound, and he rose to his feet; then the foregone conclusion which he had been in possession of ten minutes before, came back to him in its entirety. Used to every theatrical trick, he assumed facial contortion to express the extremest anguish of terror, and with one hand a little behind him, clutched the table on which flared the lantern.

"Fearest thou me?" rolled from the spectre's lips in terrible accents.

"'No!' gasped Léonce, extending a rigid hand, and pointing into the corridor with a long fore-finger. 'Grand Dieu! it is the *ghost behind you* that I fear! It advances! —it is close upon you!—there is Death upon its face!' His well-trained voice sank to a hoarse and rattling whisper.

"The apparition made no effort to turn and look behind it into that long and gloomy gallery. It shuddered for an instant, like a ship in a hurricane, then tumbled headlong to the ground. As the gruesome swathings fell from round its face and jaw, Léonce saw that he was human, and, moreover, recognized him.

"Léonce raised him—he was speechless; ran for and obtained assistance—he was dead. Whether killed by the force of the blow upon his forehead, or by the force of his own boundless and causeless terror, or a combination of both, was never known, and never will be known, 'jusqu'au jour ou tout parlera.'

"The elder student's dog was found beneath the woollen table-cloth, awaiting his dead master's word of command to move; for the practical-joking ghost was the elder student."

"Capital!" said Angela, with some energy.

" You do not ask me if I am indebted
to my own imagination for it," he remarked,
with a smile.

" No, I feel that you were not."

" You are right; it is really quite true.
And now tell us one in return."

" I will not," said Angela, ingenuously,
" because I should invent mine, and therefore you would not care to hear it."

" No," said Bertie, emulating her frank-
ness, " I have no appetite for ghost stories
that are not vouched for as being perfectly
true."

" Then, of course, I shan't relate one,"
said Angela, sulkily, " if you tell me that
you will not like it."

" I am afraid that it would not *fetch* me."

" How can one 'fetch' you ?" she inquired, not without a sentimental inflection
of voice.

Adrian looked disgusted.   " What a
beastly slang word you have taught her,
Bertie," he said.

" I think that tone of voice very fetching," Bertie replied to his cousin, without
attending to his brother.

But Angela turned upon Adrian instantly. "Do you think 'beastly' a gain upon fetching?" she asked.

"You have not repeated it after me as if you intended to adopt it," he returned.

"Indeed, no. Here is tea; then it must be five o'clock. How the ghost stories have made Time shorten himself. Let me see, Bertie, was I offended with you, or not, because you would not have my own ghost story? Yes, I was; and I will pour out tea, and you shall not have sugar. I notice that you generally abstract two more lumps after you have tasted your tea."

She ran to the ugly little wooden table —very different from those round and *club*-shaped jewels of upholstery—which every afternoon was produced from a hiding-place behind the door by old Stainer; was unfolded, had its shaky legs made as much of supports as possible, and, before it had time to tumble down, was steadied by the deposit on it of the heavy tray, that Stainer managed should balance it, after the fashion of a rope-dancer's weighty pole.

"Are you not going to give me some?" asked Adrian, as, having helped her sister, Bertie, and herself, Angela began daintily to sip.

"Pardon; I forgot you. Do you take cream—or rather milk"—peeping into the jug—"and sugar?"

"Neither."

"A 'Heathen Chinee!' How are your nerves?"

She carelessly poured the tea into the cup, and left it for him to take. He did so, looking fixedly at her, as though her face were merely a transparent case to the mechanism of her mind, a mechanism which required study.

Angela unconcernedly turned her profile. "Now how am I in profile?" she said, with her chilly little laugh.

Adrian, without replying, walked away from her.

At this point, a strong puff of eau de cologne entered the room, followed by Miss Lawless. Clemence started up, like an electrified eel, from Aunt Maria's chair.

Bertie retreated still farther from the fire, Adrian hastily laid down a pretty gold letter-weight, with which he had been playing, for it was a special pet of his aunt's, who was perpetually weighing her letters and newspapers, and would have endured a night of torment to think that she had put on a half-penny's worth more of stamp than was needful.

Miss Maria ensconced herself, and began promptly : " Angela, I hope that you have not been walking through the park in those thin boots ?"

" I have, indeed ; they are the thickest boots I ever owned in my life."

" No wonder, then, that you are so pale."

" It is not boots, believe me, that make me so."

Miss Lawless took up a book. Angela ostentatiously extended her slight feet on a footstool in front of her, and surveyed them with complacency.

" Shall I give you a cup of tea, Aunt Maria ?" said Clemence.

" I do not approve of tea, on account of
the tannin."

" But shall I give it to you ?" asked
Clemence, puzzled.

" Oh, no."

" What is tannin ?" demanded Angela.
" Will you please tell me what it is, Aunt
Maria ?"

" It is a leathery substance, formed by
the combination of tea and milk, very in-
jurious to the coats of the stomach."

"Coats !" repeated Angela; "that sounds
masculine.   Do you go to Poole, Aunt
Maria ?"

Miss Lawless   stiffened   herself, and
drenched her handkerchief afresh before
replying.   " I do not think that needs an
answer, my dear."

" No," said Angela, looking a little
ashamed of herself, " I don't think it does.
Do you know any ghost stories, Aunt
Maria ?"

" Certainly I do ; several."

" Oh, give us one !"

She shook her head, and taking up a

volume of sermons, plunged into its contents.

It was an aggravating way of hers, to pursue her religious readings in places where she was liable to distraction and interruption, and to make the distracters and interrupters smart with a sense of their offence.

Now she sat among those four young people, conscious that, when she entered the room, they were all chattering like teeth on a frosty morning, and that she had silenced and was boring them with her hard, old face, and her ostentatiously-held good book.

After ten tiresome minutes, Angela, making a little grimace to her cousin Bertrand, jumped up from her seat, and went noiselessly out of the warm morning-room into her own cold bedroom. An hour later, Clemence found her there, seated by the window, her blue fingers clasped round her knees, upon which lay a volume filled with her own girlish scribblings, partly diary, partly effusions of a *sans* back-bone character, and with a conspicuous absence of the art of prosody.

"What a 'happy family' we are, in the menagerie sense of the word, Clemence," she began at once. "I am a white Persian cat, you are a common English rabbit——"

"Oh, don't bother me with such nonsense!" said Clemence, a little impatiently; "you *do* talk such nonsense sometimes."

"Nonsense is a product of advancement, don't you see, Clemence. Man, in a primitive state, of course, had enough to do in talking of the hardest and baldest facts—they were such novelties to him—but as fact and sense became a little used up, and stale, and flat, why, of course, some clever originators introduced fiction and nonsense, and, like other weeds, they ramped, and spread, and became ineradicable; and mankind took kindly to them, and they took kindly to mankind, and so long as mankind runs his race, I suppose they will run it with him. Ah, yes; they are sure to keep pace with the double-quick of progress. The gong!—thanks, brazen one. I find myself the happy possessor of an appetite. Are you ready, Clemence? Come, then."

CHAPTER VI.

A HORSE: AND A HORSE-SOLDIER OF THE NINETEENTH CENTURY.

"THIS is spring; ethereal mild-ness!" said Angela, shiver-ingly, on Monday morning, as she finished dressing.

She looked disapprovingly out of the window as she spoke at the misty moist atmosphere which was causing the ragged rhododendrons, edging one of the walks, to droop with an increased air of dejection.

"Drink your tea at boiling-point, then put on your warmest jacket, and gallop over the lawn—on your own feet, I mean," suggested the practical Clemence.

Angela condescended not to inform her sister that she heard her speak, but tying a black scarf round her shoulders, and looking out frostily over her little standing frill, opened the door and left the room.

At breakfast some excitement was caused by Bertie's announcing his intention of riding over to see a pair of horses that had lately been in the possession of a neighbouring squire, and now were owned by a farmer who lived some five miles off, who, in his turn, wished to sell them. Bertie made it evident that he should be the probable purchaser, looking at his father with resolution as he did so.

"Come to me — ha — after breakfast, Bertie," said Mr. Lawless, in palpable distress of mind.

Bertie complied, and what the result of the interview was they knew not. Bertie was seen to mount Elspeth and ride away, and though Angela darted out to speak to him, she was too late, and returned disappointed. Adrian had gone back to town early that morning, but on Wednesday was to come again for the Easter recess.

Angela, seating herself in the most distant corner of the room, began scribbling in her diary with a fanciful gold pencil, shaped like a pistol. Clemence produced a handkerchief, that she straightway began to embroider. Miss Lawless, having closed her Church-service with a dull thud, rose up to prepare for her morning walk.

With her skirts hitched up until they presented the singularly graceful appearance of being much longer in front than behind, with her gentlemanly-looking umbrella, and her bonnet with the sprangling purple flower (which the Flora of every country should have disowned), she was presently to have been seen promenading amongst the unhappy-looking rhododendrons, with a martial tread.

Bertie did not make his appearance at lunch, and Angela was observed to be petulant.

Shortly after luncheon Mrs. North was announced, and the sisters found themselves being presented to their clergyman's wife, a pale and fragile creature, with pretensions to an exquisite tact and great charm of manner, but none to beauty.

The two young women were captivated with her in ten minutes ; she, in her turn, gratified by their ready appreciation of her inconspicuous, yet subtle graces, was inclined to be almost equally captivated with them.

" Mr. North would have done himself the pleasure of coming with me this afternoon," she said, as she rose up to depart, " but most unhappily he was called away to one of his most distant parishioners who is ill, and needed him. I wish he could have come with me ; youth and gaiety are so refreshing to a man who is wearied with brain and heart-work. It would be very good of you if you would come over and take a cup of tea with us to-morrow afternoon," she went on, addressing herself to Miss Lawless. " My boy—my son is coming home to-night on a few days' leave, and I think he will bring a friend with him.   It will be very nice of you if you will come over."

"It will be very nice for us," answered Clemence, warmly, and then, having made and received one or two more little speeches, Mrs. North took her leave.

"Well, Bertie," said Clemence, inquiringly, as her cousin entered the room an hour or two later, "have you bought the horses?"

"My father forced me to a compromise," he replied, not too good-temperedly. "I was to buy one horse, and keep the pair of weedy Methuselahs that have been in the stable for the last seven years. You can't ride together; for I think any man who would bestride one of the carriage-horses (save the mark!), would be guilty of oppressing the aged and poor, to say nothing of the ignominy of such a position. Why, riding a monkey backwards would be child's play to it! I have bought a chestnut that seems to me to be a good thing. A light chestnut, almost sorrell. I tried her, and liked her paces, and got a vet. to look her over. He pronounced her to be sound, and I could see that she was free from blemish. The man says she is a clever hunter—that's as may be—she is young, and seems almost as fanciful and sensitive for a horse as *you* are for a woman, Angela."

Angela blushed and smiled.

" Then, unless she already has a name, perhaps you will name her for me."

" No, name her ' Moonshine,' " said Fox, who had entered the room a few minutes ago.

" She is a good colour to be named Moonshine," returned Bertie.

" Then let it be Moonshine !" said Angela, with a frown, "by all means. It was very forward of me to propose having my own name given to your horse, Bertie."

" She will be far more yours than mine," he answered, with some resentment, " for I shall always ride Elspeth, of course. All right then, she shall be Moonshine, for at present she is only the ' Wild Rose filly.' I particularly asked if she had ever

been ridden by a lady, and Rayner told
me yes ; his daughter, a girl of fifteen, had
been riding her every day for the last six
months. Then he had a side-saddle put
on her, and little Miss Rayner was spirited
from the poultry-yard, and hoisted up in
her crinoline and red woollen gown, and
she went off in capital style, the filly be-
having with the gentleness of a lamb and
the manners of a fine lady. She is to be
sent over to-morrow morning bright and
early. I hope you will like her."

"I shall like to *look* at her very much
indeed," said Angela, who had recovered
her lost equanimity, "and Clemence will
like to get on her back, I dare say."

Clemence looked most brilliantly expec-
tant of pleasure from the new mare.

"Then I will give her a long trial to-
morrow afternoon, and Clemence shall ride
her first——"

"No, Bertie, you cannot go to-morrow
afternoon," said Angela, dictatorially, "for
Mrs. North was here this afternoon, and
we are all to go to tea to-morrow. I said

that I was sure you would be charmed. Why your Henry North is to be there; would you do anything but go?"

"Is Henry to be at home? I will go then, and Moonshine can be tried afterwards. Mrs. North is a cheery, winning sort of woman, is she not?"

"Oh, very; we were delighted with her. She is a perfect model of tact and grace, and it is twice as admirable from her having no beauty to help her out."

Clemence was the speaker. Bertie turned to Angela to hear her verdict.

"She is, as you say, Bertie, very winning. She is the sort of woman who could talk you into believing that the sun rose in the west, or that straw was strawberries, or a coal was a diamond. Is Henry like her?"

"Strikingly, as regards his appearance; I don't know that mentally they are the same. Fox, boy, take my arm and come out on the terrace—the side away from the wind—for a few turns before dinner."

"I want to come, too," cried Angela.

"I have not been out all day. Aunt Maria and Clemence, more enterprising, have been."

"Come, then," said Bertie readily. Angela ran away, and speedily reappeared, looking as pale as a tomb-stone saint, in her black hat and wrappings. While Fox leaned heavily on his brother's arm, and also supported himself with his crutch, Angela walked at Bertie's other side, her blue eyes scarcely leaving his handsome face as she talked to or answered him. A flush, pale as a winter sunrise, stole into her cheeks, her tongue ran on gaily, she often laughed. At last, prompted by what seemed an irresistible impulse, she clasped his arm, looking into his face with a smile. "I must be commonplace enough to say, 'between two thorns,'" she said.

Clemence, who had come to the side door, and was looking out upon them, watched her with a sorrowful gentleness resting on her face. The sorrow was for herself, the gentleness for her sister. Presently she closed the door, with a long sigh. They had passed and re-passed her many times, and given her no word; they were engrossed with each other and she went unnoticed.

Henry North was a tall and plain young man, with his mother's ill-defined, ill-chiselled features; and hair, which only by the utmost courtesy and partiality, could be called auburn. His skin, Nature had intended should be fair and pale; the sun decided differently, burning him raw sienna, except for one stripe across his forehead, which was protected by his forage-cap, and was white as ivory.

He had such a melancholy face, such a pre-occupied manner, and such a far-away look in his eyes, that many people supposed him to be deaf as an adder, and shouted at him accordingly, a proceeding that entertained him very much. He approached Angela and Clemence in a leisurely fashion, and more like a valetudinarian, than the strapping, sound, and sane individual that he really was. Angela, half turning her pretty profile towards him, met him with an exaggeration of his own manner. Clemence opposed to it her own strikingly genial, and therefore dissimilar one. Yet Angela's aspect was so charmingly that of a creature breathing a rarefied atmosphere, and "made by glamour out of flowers," that Henry North, although he had a reputation for fastidiousness and nil admirari to sustain, could not help but give her a place in his estimation that no woman had ever held, and could not refrain from giving her a far longer look than it had often been any other woman's lot to obtain from him.

He introduced his friend, a yachting man of note, the fortunate possessor of fifteen thousand pounds a year. A man, who, to use his own words, "did not go in for girls, fought shy of them," and was given to adorning his yacht with married women whose husbands, or perhaps sons, were friends of his own, who could not possibly have designs on him, and whose friendship was pleasant to him.

He was a fair, good-looking fellow
whose appearance Angela found to her
mind, and accorded him a smile so broad,
that it displayed two little dimples which
paid her cheeks only angel's visits, so
seldom did she stretch her pretty lips to
their widest extent. Henry North saw,
inwardly digested, and was piqued thereat.
" By Jove!" said his worse half—his
foolish, vain, spoilt boy half—" I'll be
given those teeth and dimples, hanged if I
won't be, before she goes !"

He took the damsel a cup of tea, which
she received with civility undoubtedly, but
with little more than a side face turned to
him, and a " thanks," both of the most un-
impeachable gravity. Seating himself beside her, he devoted himself to her in an
inert clinging, star-fish kind of way that it
was impossible to elude. Not that Angela
wished the least in the world to elude it, it
was very agreeable to her, partly for its
own sake, partly because she was foolish
and deluded enough to think that it put the
unconscious Bertie in a state of tantalism.

Henry North had been stationed in Canada two winters ago, and they soon began to exchange confidences on the subject of rinks, toboginning, snow-shoeing, sleighing. Henry had been upset from a sleigh three times, sprained his wrist toboginning on St. Helen's Island, frozen his chin and one ear while snow-shoeing, and never learnt the Dutch roll. Angela had been upset once, had frozen one ear, and no chin, had had many hair-breadth escapes, but no damages in toboginning, and had learnt the Dutch roll.

"When I am in a tobogin, I scream from the time we leave the top of the hill, until we arrive at the bottom."

" Dear me ! and do you enjoy it then ?" he said.

" Oh, excessively. The very danger is exhilarating. How exciting it is just grazing a tree, just leaping a ditch, *just* not coming to grief in fact."

He agreed with her. And a community of interest became established between them at once. They seemed loath to part from the subject and one another.

" And what do you think of my friend North ?" inquired Bertie, as they took their way homewards.

" He gave me the impression of being in debt, and in love, and homesick, and hungry," answered Angela with alacrity.

" I don't think that you gave him the impression of having given you that impression," remarked Bertie.

" I hope not!" exclaimed she. " It would grate on me to feel that he thought his sleepy attentions thrown away. I like men to think that they bring their complimentary wares to a connoisseur, and a grateful recipient, even though the grateful recipient makes no return in kind."

To this Bertie accorded no reply, but hung back, until his aunt and Clemence caught him up, and watched Angela stealing over the grass in front of him, her dress carrying with it a host of little followers in the shape of loose twigs and sticks, and dead leaves, and grasses. How pretty and winning she was, he thought; and in what a rare and original fashion. She had not one grain of common sense. Perhaps to some fellow that would not matter though; she was spoilt, capricious and wilful; perhaps that same "some fellow" would be one to think perfection undesirable, unlovable, not captivating. Certainly perfection and fascination seldom go together. Then he hurried on "lighter footed than the fox," to mount and try the new horse, which had duly arrived in the morning, and been pronounced a thing that did credit to his eye and judgment. As she behaved with the utmost discretion and prettiness under him, he declared her to be quite fit for Clemence to mount the next day. And Clemence did mount her, and rode her gracefully and well. But Angela dared not get on her back. Hating herself for her cowardice, yet unable to conquer it, she would stand with Adrian day after day, wistfully watching Bertie and her sister until they were out of sight, and feeling herself punished, robbed, and ill-used. Such a frame of mind did not conduce towards smoothness of intercourse between herself and Adrian.

Stormy and rough were many of their conversations together; for, cheated of Bertie, Angela, faute de mieux, fell back upon Adrian, to whom she was antagonistic as well as to her aunt.

While Henry North's leave lasted, she amused herself with him; for Mrs. North often came in her pretty pony-carriage to take her for a drive, afterwards carrying her back to tea. On these occasions Angela left her aunt, and the equine crawlers, in the lurch, while she learnt from Mrs. North how fascination-fraught a woman can be who has not so much good looks as you could put in your eye, and from her son how danger-fraught a very ugly man can be, who is clever and beguiling by inheritance, and who has reduced the art of pleasing to a system.

When it was possible, she attached herself to Bertie. She was quite a spoilt

child enough to cry for the possession of
an embodied fancy; and failing to achieve
that possession, quite passionate and ill-
balanced woman enough to die of disappointment and chagrin. The Fates had it
that she should merge all the vagrant pre-
ferences, all the wandering fancies, all the
stray prepossessions and whimsical loves of
her earlier youth, into a passion grand and
serious, which should bias her own conduct,
and affect the destiny of herself and others,
and be in effect the life of her life.

CHAPTER VII.

"HIN IST HIN!"

SO time glided on, and the verge of early summer was reached—that loveliest season when "a fuller crimson comes upon the robin's breast," and "a young man's fancy lightly turns to thoughts of love." The season when youthful creatures' hearts are putting forth young tendrils, and the tendrils must needs have something to wind themselves about, and when older hearts ache because of the vivid—ah! too vivid—remembrance of past summer times, when the birds' notes appealed less to the ear, and more to the heart, and when early flowers could be gathered with a sense of appropriateness to self, which is gone now, never to return. Little by little, the fitness of this sweet season, in regard to ourselves, seems to vanish as the years go by. Youth, rambling in lanes full of quivering lights and shades, and damp, delicious, earthy scents, brings back handsful of flowers, and a heart full of rejoicing, and innocent pleasure in the fairness of God's Earth. Middle age, wandering in those same lanes, is apt to bring back only a bad cold, flowers that grow only in most accessible places (they are never the prettiest), and a heart full of vain regrets.

"Venture to go on a ride to-day, Angela?" said Bertie to his cousin. "I think it is now two months since Clemence began riding the new mare, and Moonshine has never once done a thing to be cavilled at; you will be as safe on her back as you are sitting there."

Angela meditated. "I should like it," she said, slowly—"oh! dear—so much. I do so envy Clemence every day when I see you jump her up in that clever way, and ride off with her. You will watch my face, to see if I am going to faint, and arrange the reins in my hand, and dispose my habit so that it will not catch, should I tumble off—and keep close beside me, and watch the horse's manners, so that if it has premonitory symptons of shying, or rearing, you can jump off and hold it; and promise not to be cross if I drop my whip (as I once did), and you have to get down and pick it up; and go only in rustic lanes, and not tell me that I don't ride one quarter as well as Clemence; and not laugh at me for being nervous, and not be nervous yourself, and not want to ride fast—will you promise me all that, Bertie? for if you will, I intend to go."

"Of course I will; promise anything you like. And when once you assure yourself by taking a good ride, and coming back safe, and with a stunning appetite, you will not need to be persuaded to go, I'll bet anything you please."

To tell how Angela wasted a useful hour in arranging herself in her sister's habit—

howshe arranged and re-arranged her flaxen
hair, with an eye to combining the becoming and the compact, how charming she
looked when at last she left her room; how
she balanced herself on the top step, and
went in pulling off her gloves, and declaring
she could not go; how she came out again,
putting them on again, and declaring that
she would go. How the whole family
(servants at upper windows included) assembled to see her start; how she peremptorily insisted on their vanishing. How,
finally, she was lifted up by Bertie, how
absurd she was in her twitter of nervous-
ness when once on Moonshine's back; and
how, at last, she went off at a snail's pace.
All this has taken long enough in the bare
mention, and, to be enlarged upon, would
fill a chapter.

It was a lovely day. After she ceased
to hear the frightened beating of her own
heart, and knew that her hands and lips
trembled less, Angela felt attuned to it.
There was an exhilaration in being mounted,
and feeling conscious of looking fairer than

the May flowers, and of having undivided
possession of her cousin in those peaceful
lanes where they were peeped at by num-
berless " little Cyclops with one eye,"
nodded to in a friendly way by fox-glove,
in myriads ; sighed to, and whispered to,
by the young green leaves overhead which
had but for little time been open to the
light. Told a short and simple story that
began and ended with love, by the many
bird-voices which made the air teem with
primitive music, as the early spring flowers
made it teem with primitive perfume.

" If a day in early summer could only
typify life !" sighed Angela. " A rosy
dawn, a breezy mid-day, a still, and scented,
and golden afternoon, with long, bright
hours, and long, cool shadows, and bars,
and bars of amber sunshine, then a crimson
sunset, and a short, gray, quiet evening,
and the day over. What bliss that would
be ; eh, Bertie ?"

" No one has ever given an experience of a
life like that to the world," he answered,
" and therefore who can tell whether it

would be more desirable than the chequered, and stormy, and dull, and rainy ones that fall to our lot. A life like this very pretty day is not in the scheme for us. Still, my cousin, I can hope that yours will be as much like it as it is possible. Some fellow writes that 'into all lives some rain must fall;' may yours be as droughty, and sunshiny as anybody's can well be."

"What do you and Clemence talk about when you ride together?" she asked, irrelatively.

"That is one of the unanswerable questions everybody asks," he replied. "How can I possibly remember? Every manner of subject has been touched on, I believe. Clemence is very sensible."

"Oh dear! yes; she is one of that sort of people to whom all kinds of obsolete old proverbs can be applied. She would always 'make hay while the sun shone;' be 'early to bed and early to rise;' be 'the early bird that catches the worm.' For my part, I consider that bird a knave, and the worm a fool."

"You are very complimentary to your sister, Angela."

"I believe I meant to be half-complimentary to her when I began to speak, but as I finished I had forgotten her. Am I sitting square?"

"A little more to the right, and farther back in your saddle."

"Is that better?"

"Much better."

"We are to dine at the Norths' to-night, remember; Henry has come home for Sunday."

"Take care that from calling him Henry so constantly, behind his back, that you do not slip into calling him it to his face."

"I should not be very angry or shocked at myself if I did."

"I should be very angry to hear you."

"Oh! Bertie, should you? Then I shall infallibly do it. I should like to quarrel with you, only for the pleasure of making friends with you afterwards."

"But suppose I would not make friends with you?"

" Then it would be almost as great a pleasure—though of a totally different sort —to be melancholy and miserable because I was at variance with you. I should soon cry and starve myself into being so pathetically ugly that you would relent merely for the sake of beautifying me."

" A work of supererogation."

"Oh ! you should see me when I am unhappy."

" I hope devoutly that I never may do so."

"What, not even if you were the disturbing cause ?"

" My dear child, no ; that would be ten times harder for me to see. Why, what do you take me for ?"

" ' A traveller from the cradle to the grave,
Through the dim night of this immortal day,'

as I am myself; and we immortal travellers indulge in such ugly propensities by the way. We don't, in the least, mind beholding a fellow-voyager clothed in figurative sackcloth and ashes, although we pretend that we do. Bertie, I am afraid I should enjoy seeing you unhappy, and knowing myself to be the cause."

" Take care what you say——"

" Take care, for the second time within five minutes," said Angela, gravely.

" Yes, take care ; for what is said in jest often comes true in earnest."

" Bah ! can't you think of some more modern and original way of telling me ? You know there is nothing more hateful to me than are old saws."

" No; and if I could think of a more modern way I should still prefer the old. I like good old ways. I will say if you like though, that a time *may* come when you will be gratified by seeing me unhappy and knowing yourself to be the cause. But I would rather be made unhappy by you, than happy by most other people," he went on, looking at her with a proprietary sort of admiration, quite free from any special warmth, however. He had not in

the least calculated the effect of his words;
she looked so pretty, that it seemed as if
she deserved to have a pretty speech made
to her; and he was not averse to making
pretty speeches; nor was he in the habit
of weighing his words.

He never knew—he never knew, that
this afternoon's episode struck out the key-
stone of his life, and left him in after-time
with a "wounded name." Poor Bertie!

He bent a little towards his cousin as he
spoke; and on that, Angela's face grew
suddenly grave, yet at the same time
bright, and took on a look which plainly
said, "It has come then, at last!" It was
the face of a woman not in the least
startled, and quite, quite happy, as she
said with a flower-like droop of the head
towards him: "I believe I could truthfully say that to you in return." She
raised her eyes to his; they were steeped
in a light, and intensified by an expression,
which, far from intoxicating, sobered him.

For he understood with a bound of the
heart, that his cousin loved him. And she

had misunderstood him! What had he said? What had he done? Must he go on playing a part now, that her pride need not be humbled, and she rudely awakened from her strange hallucination? Foolish words! He hated them. Ah, what a gulf in our lives a few foolish words make! " And I will say it, if you tell me to do so," she continued in a half-whisper.

And although he dreaded the sound of his own voice; although he felt his heart sink as it had never done before, and his cheek grow hot with self-condemnation; although he felt all this, his want of moral courage, his faint-heartedness at causing pain, made him murmur, " Say it—if you like."

" I do like." And then she repeated his words, and they were quite silent; but with the birds carolling lays of love, and the blossoms and leaves whispering sweet messages to one another, and the light wind wooing the waving grasses and delicate wild roses with his fitful breaths, there hardly seemed to be any need for speech.

"Ah!" said Angela,—the first to speak,—"I almost feel now as if my life was going to be one long bright summer's day."

"I trust with all my soul that it may be," he answered earnestly. "Believe me, that I shall do my best, always, to make it so. I will imitate your dear sister, in smoothing and making it easy for you. She is a good sister, is she not, Angela?"

"Oh yes; of course. Tell me, Bertie, when you have been riding with Clemence have you ever wished for me to be in her place?"

A look of terrible embarrassment crossed Bertie's face, he flushed hotly as he answered, "No."

Angela's face grew crimson, and her lips quivered.

"Why should I have wished it, dear cousin," he went on, looking at her with compassion, "when I knew that Clemence was happy on the mare's back, while you would probably be unhappy? My rides with Clemence have been delightful——"

" Have I been unhappy to-day ?"

" Ah, but we have not gone off a walk yet. You don't expect to complete a ride at a snail's pace, do you ? Come, try a canter."

" No, no, I am so afraid that the canter will turn into a gallop, and I am so frightened at a gallop."

" You little muff," he answered laughing, and in a coaxing tone, " Come."

He touched his horse, and incited his companion to follow him. Angela ventured upon a canter, and finding Moonshine amenable to the feeblest touch (she could have been ridden with a silken thread) went bravely on, looking very pretty and self-pleased, and with a becoming tinge of colour brightening her somewhat pallid beauty.

It was not long before she reined up, however, for she could only talk whilst going at a walk, and she wished to be fed on the flattery of loving words. In addition she wanted Bertie to say something more definite, more tangible—something that would make of this lovely idyl a bit of the sound and unromantic prose she had hitherto found unpalatable, make a recognizable fact of the sweetest fancy that had ever occupied her visionary mind and self-engrossed heart.

" Bertie," she said timidly, " I am not in a happy dream, am I ? You are in earnest."

"Certainly; I can truthfully say that you are the sweetest creature that ever led a man's fancy captive."

"As the French Canadian children say, do you mean it, 'indeed, in double deed, across your heart and soul ?' "

" Oh, I will swear to that, by the French Canadian children, or anything else that you like."

" Thanks; I am satisfied; who could look into your face and doubt you ?"

He winced.

" Did you and Henry North ever look into the glass together as boys ?"

" Not that I remember; why ?"

" Hyperion *and* a Satyr," she returned.

" Fancy Hyperion being jealous of a Satyr."

" Did I ever say that I was jealous ?"

" Did I ever say you were Hyperion ?" she retorted with a nettled laugh.

" You implied it."

" And you implied that you were jealous, Do acknowledge that you were, the merest scrap, just to please me."

" If you know it already why should I tell you ?" he answered. " I certainly did not like the idea of your slipping into call- ing him Henry." He tried to laugh, but he looked horribly discomposed, perplexed, utterly uncomfortable.

" Then I am to take that as an ac- knowledgment ? I shall. You are so thoroughly honest and truthful, that things implied by you are as much to be be- lieved as solemn asseverations from other people."

She spoke from her heart.

" Do not make a sort of Dr. Watts of me !" he exclaimed, while a sense of igno- minious failure in sustaining the high moral

integrity that he had thought his, overwhelmed him. He felt like a man in a
troubled dream, who is slipping down
some vague decline, and who cannot go
back although it seems easy enough of ac-
complishment, and a needless and unaccountable thing to be slipping at all.

"You evidently don't like to be told my
opinion of you," she answered; "you
would rather have it left to your imagination, that you may exaggerate it into a thing
ten times better than it really is."

"Not at all——"

"Ah, well; perhaps I am judging you
by myself; but I interrupt you."

"Oh, it was of no consequence; I was
merely going to say that I would promise
not to fancy that you thought me a Crich-
ton. I don't want you to do so, Angela,
heaven knows!"

Angela looked slightly disappointed.
"Don't you?" she said, wistfully. "Then
I will not—or I will try not; but I im-
pose the law of no such wish on you, Bertie.
On the contrary, I shall be thankful for

you to think me what [I long to be—a
thousand times prettier, and cleverer, and
better."

She spoke with a little mock air of self-
disparagement, that made Bertie smile,
and say what was expected of him to
say—

" You could not be prettier, you would
be more formidable than fascinating if you
were cleverer, and what you would gain by
being better you would lose in being be-
witching ; so, if you please, I'll think of
you just as you are."

" You will turn my head," she answered
with a bright smile. " Oh, dear !" she
thought, " if I was only not 'mounted to
ride!' I can neither be graceful, coquettish,
touching, nor even at ease. I am tired,"
she said, abruptly, " let us turn, and go
home."

They did so ; and Moonshine, with her
nose pointed homewards, was a more light-
hearted and fractious thing than Moonshine
outward bound; therefore, most of the time,
until they reached Creyke, was occupied by

Bertie in encouraging and reassuring the timid horsewoman, and by the timid horsewoman in appealing to her cousin with every art of which coquettish terror is susceptible.

They reined up at the door, and, jumping off, Bertie assisted his cousin to alight. What a feather-weight she was! What fragility was hers, when compared to her sister's substantiality. And Clemence, from greater practice, could be both unfettered and graceful in her habit, while Angela, on the other hand, stumbled into the house more like an inexperienced inebriate, than an inexperienced young horsewoman.

"Have you enjoyed your ride?" asked Clemence, who was dressing for the Norths', when her sister entered the room.

"Enjoyed it!" repeated Angela, with a vigorous emphasis. "Yes; it marks an era in my life; it makes this the day of days; it is my birthday into the woman's Paradise; it has given me the realization of that which I have thought of by day,

and dreamt of by night; it has made a fact
of my dearest, most treasured fancy——
Why, Clemence, what is it ?"

For the gray look of a person in deep
mental or physical pain, had overspread
Clemence's usually glowing face.

" Nothing," she answered, with a brave
quietude. " Tell me what you mean after
we come home, and can talk unrestrainedly.
I am going to leave you now, for I know
that you like having the room to yourself,
and only by making the greatest haste will
you have time to dress."

She hurried from the room, having spoken
fast and low ; and left Angela staring after
her, with her shallow, bright blue eyes.
Presently she smiled—a smile that, though
it did not draw down her mouth at the
corners, yet had all the effect of a sneer.
Then, ringing the bell for one of the housemaids to come and help her dress, she
took off her hat, and immediately became
engulphed in a new sensation ; for a wide
crimson indentation disfigured her forehead,
and her whole mind was for the next half-

hour absorbed in efforts to make it yield to treatment and vanish. Cold cream, violet powder, toilet vinegar, glycerine, were tried in turn, with only a partial success; and to the fear that she should have to go to the Norths' with a blemish on her fairness, every other feeling succumbed.

Clemence, with a less glad and rapid step than usual, went downstairs into the drawing-room, and throwing herself into a chair near the open window, clasped her hands upon the sill, and gazed, with a profound melancholy in her eyes, out over the leafy trees and shrubs, and into the heart of the golden sunset.

It was half-past seven o'clock, and the perfect moment of what had been a very delicious day. Clemence was more unpeaceful, more troubled in spirit, wearier-hearted than she had ever been in her life; yet she doubted that she was to be made entirely miserable. Angela was at times so scatter-brained, and threw unweighed words so lavishly and carelessly to her, that she was to be pardoned for a certain scep-

ticism, that would not give under until her
sister had, as it were, authenticated herself.
But she was conscious of being very perplexed and shaken, as she sat there, looking fixedly out, yet seeing nothing that her
eyes rested on.

It was almost with the start and look of
a roughly awakened noctambulist, that she
turned at her sister's voice, and confronted
her and Bertie standing together.

"Come, we are waiting for you."

" I wonder how many imperious ' comes '
and ' goes ' you have said to me in your
lifetime ?" she answered, with her own
bright smile, and touching Angela softly
on the shoulder.

" Well, we won't stop to count now. Are
you ready ?"

" Quite ;" and Clemence took up a white
cloak that was thrown over the back of her
chair, and stood up to put it on.

" Let me help you," said Bertie, starting
forward, and taking it from her. He, too,
looked as if he might have been gazing out
over a fair summer landscape and seeing

nothing of it. Very unlike his usual self he seemed.

"Ah! well he may," she thought.

She thanked him, and tried to steal a keen glance at him unobserved by him. His hand, when for an instant it touched her shoulder, was very cold she noticed.

Then they went out of the room, and joined Miss Lawless, who was already seated in the waggonette, and waiting impatiently for them.

Mr. Lawless and Fox were to be left at home.

CHAPTER VIII.

"SAY, IS IT HEARTFELT?"

IT was the birthday of Henry, the beloved of his mother, and a party of twelve was assembled to celebrate the anniversary with their mouths and digestions.

When the Lawlesses entered the cool, rose-scented drawing-room, they found themselves the last, and dinner was instantly announced, thereby making them feel delinquents. Angela was the tardy one, and said so, in a sort of self-complimentary way. She fell to the lot of Henry's yachting friend, who was again at the Vicarage, en passant, having had Henry with him on his yacht for a day or two. Not a beautifying day or two to Henry, for he was more radiantly red than any field-poppy, and evinced an anguineal tendency to cast his skin.

The dinner was an agreeable one, for both host and hostess were charming, and the yachting man was the kind of wag who, in default of making people laugh *with* him, was satisfied if they laughed *at* him.

Henry North sought Angela directly he returned to the drawing-room, seating himself beside her with an air of appropriation that to-night seemed absurd to her.

"What a pretty woman you took in," she said ; "is she not ?"

He shrugged his shoulders, and elevated his eyebrows.

"She has about as much animation as a stuffed bird," he replied.

"But she is excessively pretty ; and look—she is going to sing now!"

The lady in question was divesting her-

self of her gloves, and with a most stolid
and unmusical face turned towards the
room, presently began to sing—

"Do not forget me ! do not forgot me !
  Think of me sometimes still ;
 When the dawn breaks, and the throstle awakes,
  Remember the maid of the mill !"

" And what do you think of that ?" asked
Henry.

" I think the song charming, the singing
of it execrable."

" Yes, it is intended to be a *song*, of
course.   One might call it a masquerading
song.   What a tone-gift it would have been
to its composer, could he only have entered
the room five minutes ago.   I see my
mother telegraphing to me with her eyes
to ask *you* to sing—will you ?"

" If you like."

" I do like ; and let it be a German song,
for German songs suit your voice best, if I
am any judge."

" I will sing 'Ich denke dein,'" rejoined
she, getting on her feet, and allowing him
to take her to the piano.   On her way

thither, she passed by two terribly disturbed faces—her sister's and Bertie's. Clemence was seated in a low chair, her head a little thrown back, her long white hands clasped loosely on her lap. Bertie was standing near her, leaning upon the high, erect back of a prie-dieu.

They were talking earnestly together, and Angela with the hopeless self-engrossment of a thorough egotist, and with the boundless imagination which was one of the delusive gifts that Fate had apportioned to her, instantly decided, in her own mind, that Bertie had flown to Clemence with a desire to confide his disapprobation of Henry North's devotion to her, and her acceptance of it. She smiled on them as she went by, and took her place at the piano, Henry North hovering over her like a gentlemanlike and well-intentioned bird of prey.

"Will not your sister come and sing a duet with you?" asked he, as Angela concluded her song.

"I dislike singing duets," she said, "and

Clemence sings so very much better than I do, that I always think it a pity for my voice to be marring the effect of hers."

" Your voice and hers are certainly of a very different timbre," he observed, " but I think they sound charmingly together. However, since you don't like duets, pray sing again alone."

" I will not, indeed," she returned ; her tiresome sensitiveness, that a touch wounded, being wounded now—" go, ask Clemence to come and sing."

" No, no ; I pray you not to do so, and implore another song."

But Angela had risen from her seat, and taken her gloves, and was looking at him with her peculiarly cold and insolent smile, while her eyes told him that she was nettled.

Thereupon, with an almost imperceptible shrug of the shoulders, he left her, advanced a few steps towards Clemence, but saw in an instant that some point of deep import was being discussed between the cousins, and, wheeling round, returned to

Angela, who had been narrowly observing him.

"Really," he said, "I do not like to break in upon your sister's conversation, for it is so evidently of a profoundly interesting nature."

Angela laughed.   "I would wager all my large possessions that I know what they are talking about," she replied.

"What, pray?" he inquired, with some curiosity, and watching Clemence's grave, bright-hued face, rather than Angela's laughing white one.

"About me."

"Oh! then I hope that the depression visible on Bertie's countenance does not strike deeper."

"You are quite detestable and unlike yourself to-night," said Angela; "you know that I do not depress Bertie or any one else."

"The thought of you depresses me, I assure you, when I am present in the body, in my grilling-machine of a tent at Alder-shot, and am longing to be bodily with my absent spirit. If all the regrets, and heart-burnings, and jealousies, and miserable longings, and aching disappointments that even one very charming woman has caused, were to assume visible form, and array themselves before her startled eyes, what a formidable host they would be!"

"Yes," answered Angela, who always preferred, and was more fully prepared to fancy things that were impossible, rather than to think of those that were not, "but it would not prevent her doing her very best to have that accusing host arrayed before her. To be the cause of the deepest pain a man is capable of, that is what a woman most desires, I believe. She prizes it far more than a corresponding amount of love. For a man to love her and be happy is pleasant, but a little tame. For a man to love her and be exceedingly unhappy, is delightful to her."

"I hope that all women are not like that, however," answered young North a little sceptically.

Now Angela practically knew very little

of masculine or feminine human nature, and although feeling thoroughly capacitated to reply that all women *were* like that (according to the ideas evolved out of her inner consciousness), deemed it better not to commit herself, and was silent.

"I don't think that your sister would be that kind of person," he said, abruptly, forced, as it were, into recognizing a womanly honour and grace of feeling by the proximity of Clemence's face, and the singularly lovely and admirable expression at that moment beautifying it.

"Clemence?" echoed Angela, in great astonishment; "no, I dare say not. She would blow out the candle and leave herself in the dark, in a thunder-storm, rather than see an obstinate moth commit felo de se. When we were children, I used to catch flies and put them in hungry spiders' webs, and she would take them out again just as the spider was about to pounce. She is a dear and good creature, my sister, and was born to take care of me, I verily believe."

" Selfish, pretty little midge," thought North, looking at her in admiration tempered by disapprobation.

" Don't flatter yourself that is all the share she is to have in the grand scheme," he said. " Before you know where you are, some fellow will be assuring himself, you, and her, that she was made for the express purpose of taking care of *him.*"

Angela laughed with a sort of lazy tolerance of his absurdity.

" It might happen, yes," she thought, but long after she herself was happily disposed of, and needed no further care at her sister's hands.

" If you are so ablaze with admiration of my sister's excellences, why have you hitherto kept it under a bushel ? Why have you not been nice to her as you have been—have been—well, to me ?"

" Because you are twice as pretty, and ten times more amusing," was his mental reply. Aloud, he said, "Can you ask why? Who sees the stars by sunlight ?"

" If that is a conundrum, I give it

up.   If it is a tribute, I thank you; astronomical compliments are always favourites. The sun, moon, and stars are in even greater request when a pretty speech is to be made, than roses, lilies, and violets, or any description of bird or beast."

" If my speech was a pretty one, it was a particularly ambiguous one," he rejoined, in his emotionless, musical voice; "and it is quite like your usual kindness to take it at its best.   Here comes Osborn over to talk to you ; I wish he were farther and faring worse; but I shan't leave you to a tête-à-tête with him.   Do you hear me ?"

" Oh ! yes ; I hear ; do not.   I shall be very glad for you to stay."

Indeed she would be.   She would have liked to collect about her every male thing in the room (there were six), four of them she presently did monopolize.   Bertie and Mr. North were the two exceptions.

" Clemence," Bertie said to his cousin, immediately on his return to the drawing-room, " has Angela yet said anything to you ?"

" She has told me that she is very happy," replied Clemence, quietly; "and I know very well why she is so."

" What can you think of me ?—but there is only one thing to think, and that is what I think of myself—that I am a pitiable combination of fool, and knave, and sneak. Yet my words—Clemence, how can I say it ?—she is your sister, and my cousin. My words misled her most unhappily. You see, she is so much in the habit of fancying things; and I did not think—I did not mean——"

Clemence held out her hand with an imperious movement to him to stop.

" I cannot be silent," he went on, flushing crimson. " The instant I had said what I did say—I'll tell you exactly what it was—I felt that I had committed a folly and a blunder, that would come to be chargeable to me as a deep offence. She must be made to understand how it is—Clemence, for heaven's sake, help me; tell her how it really is."

" But I do not know myself ' how it really

is.' You have been a very dear and charming cousin to me."

"Clemence! when you know that I love you!" he exclaimed reproachfully.

She smiled sadly. "Yes, Bertie, *when* I know that you do, it will be time enough, quite, to give Angela the cruel benefit of that knowledge."

"Then the time is now. The hours that I have spent with you in these long bright afternoons can never be unspent; and the lesson learnt in them never unlearnt, and the heart given away in them never taken back again. Clemence, you have it; it's yours through life and death, not Angela's, not any one's but yours. You are my cousin, my love; my wife that must be or I will have none."

"I cannot hurt Angela," murmured Clemence, with the dark-fringed eyelids drooping over her tender gray eyes. "Never, never! She is happy in the belief that you—oh, most cruelly!—have caused her to have. I blame you, Bertie," she

said, with grave simplicity, and lifting her
eyes suddenly to his face.

" Blame me ? that is gently said. I
execrate myself. Yet Angela must know
that I meant nothing beyond the wondering admiration that she extorts from every
man. Tell me, Clemence, do you care for
me ?"

" I shall not answer you," she rejoined,
with a resolute shake of the head.

" Good heavens ! don't let me think that
you intend to be one of those monstrously
mistaken ones, who do not scruple to sacri-
fice themselves, and the man who loves
them, for the sake of giving another
woman the hollow, rotten satisfaction of
marrying that same man, who to them is
unloving. Don't tell me that you are
going to immolate me upon the altar of
sisterly affection."

Clemence was silent, weighing probabili-
ties carefully in her mind ; while Bertie,
rigid with suspense, waited for her to
speak again.

" No," she said at last, "they _are_ mistaken ones ; I will not be one of them. I will not give you up to Angela, much as I love her. Bertie, this is true that you have told me ? It is heartfelt ?"

"No wonder that you do not believe me," he said, gloomily, "I don't deserve to be believed. Yet, nevertheless, I *am* to be. Your feminine acumen—-instinct— whatever it should be called—must have told you long ago that I love you. Now my lips repeat what my heart has so often said, and I am to be believed. You are my first love, and will be my last. You are 'nobly planned;' you have a heart so tender, deep, and true, that a man would need no other home could he feel himself cherished in it."

"Angela," murmured Clemence, although her cheek flushed with pleasure, "I cannot allow myself to feel happy when I think of Angela, who by my happiness must be made miserable. Bertie!" she went on, with a swift and sudden inflection of anger in her voice, "I realize!—you have acted a *miserable* part. You cannot really care for either of us poor sisters. Good-bye to you. I want *my own* lover; I do not want my sister's."

"*I* am not your sister's lover; I am yours."

" And what does *my sister* think ?"

He did not answer.

" You know what she thinks ; and so do I. But you do not know as I do, with what tenacity she can cling, and with what passionate fervour she can attach herself to her own fancies ; and this is not a fancy; you have made it a reality to her. My dearest cousin," and her voice softened irresistibly, " for your own sake, and for hers, and for mine, you must learn to love her."

" To do that I must first learn to unlove you ; and nothing could be more impossible than that," he said, with vehemence. " Tell her so."

" It would sound selfish and cruel! I cannot. She would never forgive me."

" Then I must; and I would rather be bastinadoed."

"You will not find the courage," said Clemence, with a slight, sad smile. "When alone with Angela, and looking into those dazzling blue eyes of hers, you will never have the courage to say to her, ' I did not mean what I said to you ; I do not care for you, nor shall I ever ; I am a coward ; despise me as you must, and forgive me if you can.' "

"I will," he returned, resolutely, "and you have taught me the words to use. She shall ride with me to-morrow, and she will leave the door fancying that she cares for me, and will come home knowing that she detests and contemns me. Clemence, one little word to cheer me !"

"Not one," she said, turning her face away from him. "For to-night you are Angela's, and perhaps may be always. For I tell you again, Bertie, that the knot you have tied with your own tongue, you must untie with your own teeth ; I shall do anything rather than help you. My sister has been my most precious possession ever since I can remember, and no word

of mine shall help to alienate her from
me."

"You *shall* say that you care for me—I
long to hear you—you shall !"

" Indeed I will not.   I wish some one
would come and ask me to sing.   Captain
North came towards me a little while ago
as if he was going to do so, but he retreated, and went back to Angela."

" How calmly you can go on talking,"
he said, bitterly, " while I am not even
master of my thoughts.   Yet I know that
you would not willingly torment me.
Thank Heaven for the knowledge !   Only
tell me, Clemence, do you love me, or do
you not ?"

" That is a question which every woman
is bound to answer, provided the man has
a right to ask it.   I am not bound to answer you, for you have no right to ask
me."

" Why have I not ?"

" Because you know perfectly well how
truly I love my sister ; and if you do not
know that my love for her, and my sense

of justice towards her, prevent my answering you, why learn it now."

He could not urge her.   And although many of the words she had used had been hard, the manner was so gentle in which they had been spoken, that they did not irritate him.

He bowed to her as "a perfect woman nobly planned," he, in his own estimation, seeming to be a most imperfect man, very ignobly planned.

Then they came and asked her to sing, and going to the piano she sang with consummate grace and feeling, "Say, was it heartfelt?" and Bertie, listening and watching her fine and noble face, answered the vocal appeal in his heart with a strong affirmative.

Angela, having at last said good-night to the imperturbable and persistent Henry, took her place in the waggonette.

"Are you very angry?" she whispered, with an air of exhilaration about her, to Bertie, by whose side she had placed herself.

"With myself? yes," he answered gravely.

Poor little blinkard! How little she comprehended his meaning. How she devised out of his words a flattering tribute to her own power over him.

" Do not be," she said, coaxingly. "I suppose you mean that you are angry with yourself for caring, because Nature has made me a coquette. I can't help it. And men are such fools, you know——"

" They are."

" You are not !" she breathed into his ear, earnestly. " You are a lion amongst jackals."

He turned away from her, saying hastily to old John :

" Hold up ; I want to get out—and smoke," he added, to his aunt and cousins. " Aunt Maria will not let me smoke here ;" this last in reply to a vexed and disappointed look from Angela.

" There is nothing that I should like so much to do as to walk across the park in this lovely half moonlight," said Angela, eagerly.

But Bertie apparently did not hear her, for he made no reply, going off alone at a quick pace.

" Quite a proper ending to so blissful a day," said Angela, after they entered their room.

She pushed Clemence gently away from the lighted glass, that she might examine her own happy face.

" I hope my head will not be turned. Mr. Ruthven has asked me to let him name a horse that is to be a famous steeple-chaser, after me. Mr. Vane is going to make Uncle Francis let me go for a little cruise on his yacht ; you too, I dare say. As for Henry North, you see how *he* is Bertie is *mine*. Oh, you poor Clemence" (with a compassionate look, under which Clemence winced), " drink vinegar, dye your hair fair, live on bon-bons and pastry, and perhaps that aggressively healthy look will wear away, and you will fine down, and——"

" I don't want to fine down," said Clemence.

" But don't you want to be the kind of thing that men prefer ?

> " ' Like a lily which the sun
> Looks through in his sad decline.' "

" Most of them do not prefer it," answered Clemence stoutly. " The Byronic passion for starved, ' ethereal ' women, languishing, sentimental beings, is quite old-fashioned, and *ridiculed* now. They don't prefer it."

" Oh, don't they ?" returned Angela with a little incredulous shrug, and a long look in the glass, followed by a triumphant smile. " Well, perhaps you are right. I did not think Bertie was capable of such absurd jealousy as he has shown to-night. Do you know he would hardly speak to me this evening. You noticed that, I suppose? And shook hands just now, when he said good-night. Foolish, jealous, dear boy. I love him all the more for being so tenacious of his rights ; but can't you see what a temptation it is to tease him ?"

" No."

"Heavens! I did not know that two letters could be made to sound so sepulchral. What has gone amiss with you, Clemence? I noticed something odd about you when I came in this afternoon. Are you angry with me because I am so happy?"

"Oh, no, no."

"If I ever get the reins here, how I shall idealize this place. It has all the rudiments of beauty. What will Uncle Francis think of this, I wonder? I do not believe he will object very much. And then he is powerless, you know. Oh, I am a staunch upholder of the law of primogeniture. Dear old Francis is tied by the leg, as regards the entail. He can make it nasty enough for us while he lives; but I believe I can cajole him into good-nature—don't you think it?"

"No."

"You are prodigal of negatives to-night."

"I am sure that nothing is yet definitely arranged between you and Bertie, Angela."

" Oh, he has been confiding his affairs to you, has he ? One of the ill-effects of his friend Henry North. No; nothing is *coup-sur* yet. It is in that intermediate state than which nothing can be more delicious. It will not be half so charming when it is bruited abroad, and one is beringed and betrothed."

" Wine poured out is not swallowed," said Clemence, taking refuge among her stock of proverbs.

" To the scaffold with your old saws ! I hate them, and you know that I do. What can you think of yourself, to be trying to make uncertainties of my half-fulfilled hopes ? What do you mean, Clemence ?"

" Oh, Angela, dear Angela, are you sure that Bertie's love for you is more than cousinly ?"

" You detestable, insulting, ill-natured, envious, 'proud sister'—you deserve the plurality of epithets I have given you. Leave the subject alone, please. I will not be *very* angry with you, because——I am sorry for you."

" And I for you," said Clemence softly.

" Bah !" cried Angela angrily, " you are envious of me. Leave the subject alone."

" Very well."

There was a long, long pause. Then Angela suddenly broke into speech.

" Aunt Maria's dress was exquisite ! Altogether *too* exquisite for her. What a delicate mauve ! and Chambéry gossamer ! I could not help picturing how I should have looked in it. Very silly of me. It was quite lovely; no wonder that she cackled about 'what she should wear,' yesterday. *She* should wear ! Why she is as ugly as one of the nondescript animals that support the shield at the gate. If I had had my way, she should have gone in a gown made of old pudding-bags looped with mushrooms, and with a wreath of dried onions on her head."

" Then you could have worn the mauve gauze."

" Exactly; and wisterias in my hair. Oh, how tired and sleepy I am; pray do not talk to me any more; if you do, I shall

be snappish with you, I warn you." And
Angela nestled her head down upon the
pillow, bade her sister put her watch at the
head of the bed, and extinguish the candle.
Clemence obeyed her, and sought her own
couch in silence and darkness, and with a
heavy heart.

CHAPTER IX.

OLL was rejoicing in the sunshine, down by the mill-pond. And her rejoicing took the form of a song that had no longer scale than a blackbird's whistle, and a dance, whose measure was trod no more gracefully than were the gambols of the long-legged, short-bodied lambs in the neighbouring meadows.

Doll was meditating a frolic a little later on in the day, in those same meadows, which were sprinkled thick with daisies, "pearled Arcturi of the earth." Were there not colts in them, with legs even more preposterously lengthy than the

lambs'? If Doll had a passion for anything in the world, it was colts. Two of
these that she was about to chase and
fondle, were not aristocratic horselings,
they were but the rough and sturdy children of rough and sturdy dams and sires;
born to the plough, and the heavy waggon,
boasting no pedigree, but very engaging,
in their extreme youth, to Doll, who was
an adept in coaxing and chasing them into
corners, and then cossetting them to her
heart's content. Stroking and kissing their
velvet noses, looking into their large
brown, bright eyes with her own, which
were nearly as brown and large and
bright.

When the miller's waggon, with its
orange body and yellow wheels, went lumbering away, Doll also departed, and went
up the lane at a dog-trot; yet pausing at
intervals to pluck the largest, most velvety,
and greenest clovers, such as she fancied
would be prized by the equine palate.
Under the shade of the leafy elms, where
a spring, trickling musically, bathed them,

grew the biggest and best; these she gathered: forming them into a kind of nosegay.

They were a love-offering to the oldest colt of the three; a little creature as to whom a passing rustic had stabbed Doll to the heart only a week ago by saying that "it war good for naught; and had best have had the bullet through its brain a goodish bit ago, that it must soon have: for it war good for naught."

It was malformed. Its fore hoofs, instead of being of the orthodox "horse-shoe" shape, were prolonged, turned upwards, uneven and rough, like an old man's shoe. It was, because of them, a monstrosity. Doll's heart bled for this colt. While the other foals, babies still, gambolled about the thick-set, rough-hided, lumbering mares their dams, he, already arrived at equine hobbledehoyhood, stood still looking at them out of his brilliant hazel eyes, in which Doll fancied that she could see a sorrow for himself.

His mother was no thick-legged, heavy-headed cart-horse; she was a "ladye of high degree," dainty and sleek; and was separated from her little son, and forgot him. He, with his delicate head, and his rudiment of a perfect form, was a failure; and in the daisied field hobbled with pain and difficulty, and watched the foals of the rude brood mares gambolling and frisking at their will. Poor little colt! Doll's heart grieved for him.

It had been a pleasant moment to her, when, having chased him round the meadow, she had easily hemmed him into a corner, and had made his eyes change their look of dilated terror to one of pleasure and confidence, as she fed him with a handful of hardened oatmeal porridge, saved from her own spare breakfast; and, smoothing his black mane, kissed his soft tan muzzle, calling him fond and pitying names, and loving him because he was worthless, and half-helpless, and altogether different from the other two lusty foals who, with their mothers, shared the field with him.

Every day she went to the meadow, and every day since meeting the farm-hand her heart had beaten so that she could hear it, fearing that the colt would be no longer there. To-day was no exception. Any one watching Doll as she came within sight of the meadow, would have seen a look of tension, almost of distress, creep over her pretty brown face, as, with a contraction of lids and brows, to see the farther, she peered over the hedge, to assure herself of the little creature's presence or absence.

He was there! Doll's fingers, that had relaxed their hold of the bunch of juicy clover, now tightened it; and she sprang over the wire fence, and privet hedge, and made for the object of her affection, who was standing quietly, with his charming head erect, and his black mane blowing in the soft summer wind.

He pricked up his ears as he descried Doll and her green bouquet, and, dragging his great fore-feet clumsily along, did his poor best to meet her half-way.

"Coltie, coltie," said Doll, in the tenderest accents ; and while she separated his mane with her brown fingers, she held the bunch of clover for him to nibble and devour, and called him a "pet," and a "duck," and a "dear," for Doll's vocabulary of endearing epithets was a limited one.

As she had become fonder of this little creature, her attentions to the two foals had considerably diminished, and to-day she only watched them flourishing their spindle hind legs in the air, or lying flat upon their sides asleep in the sun, and contented herself with talking to, and caressing the little cripple.

By certain little signs and tokens Doll managed to have a sketchy notion of how time was going, and, as her father counted on her to be at home when he came, to make and pour out his tea for him, she was very nearly certain to attend to his wishes ; for they were usually wishes in the imperative mood, and contravention to them he occasionally made visitable with a cuff, or a push, or a coarse—and I must in justice say, an unmeaning—oath.

She turned more than once to look back at her four-footed *miserable*, and was gratified to observe that he watched her intelligently and regretfully until she was out of sight.

It was a day worthy of Eden before temptation entered in; balmy, perfumed; the air gently in motion, yet not windy. The smoke ascending straight and quivering, the sunbeams lying slanting and still over the buttercups and dry, bright grasses, gilding the homely gray of the hay-ricks, flecking the mill-stream with golden rays and lozenges. And Nature at her best was not dumb; in the voices of a thousand birds she told her sweet, yet pitiless story :

"Such as I seem to you to-day, mortal, I seemed to your twice great-grandsire, as he took his way along the path that your feet are treading now, and so will I seem on just such another day to your great-grandson. Your father's father's father, and you, and your son's son's son are all alike to me. I will smile on your dead and bloodless face as kindly as I smile upon your living and lusty one. My tens of thousands of birds sang a century ago as they sing now, and as they will sing a century hence. My countless young leaves thrill and sigh, and my west wind woos them to-night as it did a decade ago, or will a decade from now. The great agent, I am relentless and unsympathetic; yet, nevertheless, in every generation I have my innumerable adorers. Insensate is he who does not lay the love-offering of a softened mood, a tribute of deepest, most wondering admiration, at my universal shrine."

Doll, in after-years, recollected the fulvid light, and the scented air, and the fresh waving green of that early summer evening. The Doll that then was, had only an imperfect knowledge that the face of nature was that evening very fair : and " *Sursum corda,*" a faint voice said to her in an unknown tongue.

She began to sing out of very light-heartedness; and, singing, turned her back upon the meadows, with their grazing flocks and ruminating kine, and upon the topaz sunset, and crossing the strong old bridge over the stream that here began to swell into a river, entered the shady village street. In an instant, her quick eyes fastened upon a pair of equestrians coming at a walk over the uneven stones. In one, she recognized Mr. Bertie Lawless, the squire's heir. In the other she recognized nothing of such humanity as it had been her lot hitherto to be brought in contact with. Nor was this person of such stuff as Doll's dreams were made of. For Doll drew only upon past experiences in her wanderings in the " Debatable Land."

She saw a face whiter than the chalk at the village school; and from that face looked a pair of eyes, very large, and very vividly blue and bright. The young lady seemed hardly to be enjoying herself; she sat forward, and up in her saddle holding the reins and whip as one who would gladly be without them. Her tall hat had slipped back, leaving visible much more disordered fair hair than was seemly.

It was Angela, of course ; taking her second ride upon Moonshine, and in consequence of the mare's unexpected light-heartedness, very miserable. They had ridden five miles, yet Bertie had been quite unable to maintain anything like a connected conversation with his cousin. As for explanation, self-condemnation, or earnest appeal, it was totally out of the question ; and he could not help but feel himself reprieved.

" Oh," he said, reining up (an example which his companion was only too glad to follow), " here is the little girl I was telling you about the other day."

" What, little Miss Scare-the-birds ?" was the reply, quite audible to Doll, who reddened angrily. " I wish she would ride this creature back for me and let me walk home ; or, I suppose the village boasts *one* fly ?" she spoke pettishly. Her ride had been more penance than pleasure to her ; and Bertie had been unaccountably chilly.

"Pray ride home," he answered; "I have something most especial to say to you; something that I had planned to say before we set out."

"It curvets, and caracoles so! It did not do so yesterday, it went straight."

"You have not ridden her with so light a hand, and she resents it; and besides, for some reason or other, she *is* much fresher than she was yesterday; but it's only play; she has not an atom of vice. Clemence would enjoy her little sidelong airs and graces, for they are nothing more."

As for Doll's face, when she caught the young lady's suggestion, no words can give an adequate idea of the illumination that overspread it. That she, Doll, should actually be elevated to the back of a living horse, and placed in the orthodox position upon a real lady's saddle! No, no; out of a dream that could never be. Fulfilment of an inborn desire comes not often in a life-time; and Doll and the horse were by Destiny linked together.

Was she to be elevated to that seat,

which occupying, she would envy no throned potentate ? Capricious as the wind, Angela willed otherwise.

"Clemence!" she repeated angrily, " I wish she was in my place. Very well, since you have words of weight to say to me, I will venture back. Get out of the way, child," she cried half nervously, half imperiously to Doll, whose mouth had drooped, and whose face had lost its glow of expectation.

"Poor little chicken," said Bertie, " she thought that you were really in earnest when you spoke of her riding Moonshine home."

" And so I was *then*," returned Angela. " *Do* get out of the way, little girl—she's going to rear ! oh, help me, Bertie, she's going to rear !"

" Let go her curb," said Bertie, trying to speak very quietly, yet forcibly at the same time.

But Angela, not attending to him literally, hung on by the reins, a proceeding that the horse was not slow in resenting, snort-

ing and plunging, nearly unseating her inexperienced rider, who with no thought of
guiding her away from the immobile little
bit of humanity that stood with tear-
dimmed eyes in the middle of the street,
let her take her reckless way.

The mare's half-run-away, half-playful
bounds brought her to an opposing
object; her cruel fore-feet met the unresist-
ing air for an instant, as, with the sudden-
ness of a steel-spring she raised them, then
they met something resistant, she knew
not what, nervous and excitable creature
that she was—Doll knew what, for a throe
of keenest pain struck through her poor
brain, and her shattered side. Then to
Doll a strange, dreamless night came.
To Moonshine came a sense of having
successfully beaten down that opposing
object, and of being galloping ventre-à-
terre, down the rough resounding street,
with a shrieking something on her back.
To Bertie came a sickened horror. The
terrible picture burnt itself upon his recollection of a slight, ill-clothed form lying

prone, and a brown and rosy face turning ashy and agonized as it struck sideways upon the uneven stones, quivered for an instant, and then was still ; a second picture of his cousin galloping furiously down the village street, with a sharp and terrified cry, although not horrible, was certainly somewhat alarming. Then came a vision of the doorways of the village shops quickly filling with faces ; of some one dashing out, and waving a hat at the bolting steed ; how Bertie imprecated that same incapable !

" The child !" he shouted, as he galloped past his friend, the saddler, who felt a deeper interest in the run-away horse, and the run-away-with girl from the fact that his saddle was on the back of the one, and convulsively clutched by the other.

" See to the child !" shouted Bertie, as he spurred Elspeth on. He turned his head, notwithstanding the pace at which he was going, when he neared the bend in the street, and saw forms of both men and women stooping kindly over the prostrate

child.   Then   he   raced   on   after   his
cousin.

He watched her hair break from its re-
straining pins, and uncoiling, stream flutter-
ing out like a banner of cloth of gold.   At
intervals he heard her give an hysterical
cry, and wondered why she did it; for the
road was perfectly flat and smooth, it was
only two miles to the park, and Moonshine's fleet gallop was smooth and elastic
as a deer's.   There was nothing to dread;
and for any one, who like Clemence enjoyed a burst at racing speed, there was
much to enjoy.   The road was clear as far
as eye could see, and flat as one's hand.
I am afraid that Bertie called his fair-
haired cousin a muff, as he heard her
shrieking out his name every minute or
two.   "Don't be frightened," he shouted,
"there's nothing to be frightened at.   Just
keep a firm, light hand, and sit still; she's
going straight home."

And she did run straight to her stable;
and Bertie was able, in the stable-yard, to
catch in his arms an Angela of snow,

speechless and gasping, whom he carried into the house, where Clemence promptly did everything most judicious for her sister, and before long Angela's blue eyes opened, and she welcomed herself back to consciousness with a faint exclamation.

" And I am not killed," she said; " oh, Bertie, why did you not save me ?"

" My dear Angela," he answered, "would I not willingly have done so, if I could ?"

" It was your fault, and the fault of that staring stupid child," Angela went on, raising herself upon one slight arm, while the faintest, most exquisite briar-rose pink stole over her face.

" The ' stupid child ' has almost more reason to blame you, than you her, if there is any *blame* in the case," he answered, flushing hotly.

" How can you say that ?" answered she, flinging herself back on the sofa cushions, and raising a pair of angry eyes, with a frown above them, to his face. " If you had not stopped to speak to her, and she had not terrified Moonshine, by being directly under her feet, I should never have been run away with."

" Angela !" cried Clemence, clasping her hands, " you have not run over any one ? Not a child ? Has she ?" appealing to Bertie.

Bertie briefly stated what had occurred.

" It was not my fault," said Angela, sniffing at a vinaigrette and closing her eyes. " Poor little thing ! What a pity ! Is it not dreadful ? Come up to my room with me, Clemence. Bertie, you won't mind giving me your arm upstairs, will you ? Well, if I had not been a lucky young woman, I should not be here safe and sound at this moment, eh, Clemence ?"

" I am thankful," replied Clemence, briefly, but with heartfelt earnestness. " Do you know, I think that I must send— or better still—go into the village myself, and see how it fares with the poor *un*lucky one who is *not* safe and sound. Oh, if she should be——"

Angela stopped her with a scream.

"How unfeeling you are, Clemence!" she said, as she raised herself, and taking Bertie's arm, clung to it. "Do you think that I have no nerves? no sensibilities?"

"I am not unfeeling, and you know it," replied Clemence, and there stopped short; her sister's want of heart struck her with a terrible sense of newness, and with keen pain.

As for Bertie, he looked from one sister to the other as one who intelligently, yet dumbly, separates the wheat from the chaff. He was no beauty worshipper, his warm and loving heart demanded from the object of his choice a sympathy and tenderness that Angela had it not in her power to give.

"I pictured to myself, even as I tore along like a rifle ball, twenty horrid deaths for myself," said Angela, with a faint pride in her own invincible imagination. "I fancied myself dashed against a tree. I fancied myself whirled over that steep bank just by Fermor's Cottage; I fancied Bertie coming up with me just as I swayed from the saddle, and finding that it was too late; that my poor heart had ceased to beat from sheer——"

"If you go into the village, I will go with you, but you will have to walk, for Aunt Maria has not come home yet," said Bertie, cutting her short without a particle of rudeness, but with an inattention which caused her to open her blue eyes their widest, and regard him with mingled astonishment and offence. She relinquished his arm at her door without a word.

"I am glad your bolting horse did not come to grief, Angela," he then said very kindly. "I have seen heaps of women run away with, and they never came to any harm, especially if they had such a nice flat clear road before them ; but," he went on, with an increased gravity of tone, "they never had the grievous misfortune to bowl anybody over as they went along."

Angela, turning her head away, suddenly began to shed an abundance of tears.

"Do you mean to say that you blame

me for letting that child take care of herself, and get out of the way, when it was
all I could do to take care of *my*self, and
not be thrown ? It would never have
happened, but for her. You and she have
yourselves to thank for the whole thing,
and that I have escaped with my life
seems anything but a matter for congratu-
lation to you and Clemence. You are bar-
barously cruel."

Then she stumbled into her room, and
shut the door hard, not only in his face,
but in that of Clemence, who had listened
to her in dismay.

"Angela ! Angela !" she cried shaking
the handle of the locked door, "pray let
me in ! pray do !"

There was no response; and as the
sound of sobs had altogether ceased, and a
noise of the opening and shutting of
drawers was audible, Clemence concluded
that her sister felt equal to changing her
attire at once, and so turned unwillingly
away.

"I'll get on my hat directly," she said

hurriedly to Bertie. "You'll wait for me?"

He nodded, and while she ran into her aunt's dressing-room, where she had that morning left her hat, he descended the stairs. She found him at the door, staring into space, while he absently played with the ear of Skip, a fox-terrier belonging to Fox, that had stationed itself on a wooden chair beside him.

Without speaking, they hastened down the avenue, taking every short cut feasible. It was two miles and a half to the village, but Clemence, a lithe, and strong, and active creature, made nothing of it, and turned down the lane leading to the mill, perfectly unfatigued.

John Drake, who had come home from his work to find his sadly injured and suffering Doll stretched upon his own rough bed, heard the story of the accident from the village doctor, who was attending to the child, and heard it with a species of fury.

So the squire's niece had ridden over his girl! They interrupted him to tell him that the young lady was a poor, thread-paper thing, with weak wrists, and weak nerves. He must not blame her too much. Mrs. James, the saddler's wife, who had seen the accident, was gently laying wet cloths about the child's injured head ; she was a good sort of creature, and had done all she could, and would continue to do so, she assured Drake and the doctor.

" Will the girl die ?" said John in a husky whisper, raising his head and confronting the doctor.

" No, no ; most probably not ; oh, dear, no ! in all probability not," answered Mr. Hurst reassuringly. " Two of her ribs are fractured—that is to say broken—and there is an injury to the skull—the head, but she will swing round, my friend, in time. With care, she will be quite the same bright and active lass again in due time."

Here Clemence and Bertie entered, and Bertie, going up to the doctor, said in a low voice—

" I heard those last words of yours, Mr. Hurst, and I am thankful that you are able to say them.   Drake, my good fellow," he continued to John, who with a sullen gesture turned away his head, " I feel very badly to see this cheery child lying like that ! I'd give my right hand almost for it not to have happened.   But no blame must attach to my cousin, mind, for she is nothing of a horsewoman, and could not manage her horse.   Everything that can be done for Dolly *shall* be done, that you may be sure of—everything."

Drake muttered something more inimical than grateful ; but when he caught sight of Bertie's face, bending with heartfelt distress and regret over Doll, the expression of his own rugged countenance changed and softened.

Clemence, saying " It was my sister who who was so unfortunate—you must let me do everything I can," looked at him with her deep and tender eyes, and raising Doll's brown hand very tenderly, laid her cheek softly against it for an instant.

Her tone, her looks, this little act, were all so genuine, so thorough in their kindliness, that John could not be altogether obdurate ; and he knew that he must take help, let it come from what quarter it might—it was a necessity that could not be dodged nor avoided.

Long after their dinner-hour the cousins lingered on in the labourer's mean room, watching the suffering child ; for that she did suffer, was testified by a faint moan from time to time, and the occasional quivering of her white lips.

At length Clemence said, " Shall we go now, Bertie ? I am coming again in the morning. To-night Mrs. James is going to stay—the poor child has no mother and no women relations, it seems—good of her, is it not ?"

" Not half as good as it is of you to think of coming back again," said Bertie warmly ; " for something in your tone tells me that when you come, you will stay a long while."

"I shall, for I am grieved; I cannot bear to think of her—motherless and sisterless, and with only her labourer father, who must go on all the same with his rough work, —lying here suffering by such a terrible accident. I am ready; let us go."

The foregoing conversation had been held in the outer room, which they had had to themselves; for, on Clemence's entrance, Drake had gone into the room where his daughter lay, shoeless, with the tread of a well-intentioned elephant.

Clemence and her cousin went out of the ill-conditioned room into the gloaming, and as they did so, the father, with his toil-roughened face, bent over little Doll. What a changed Doll, from the slip of pretty radiant life that had come rushing down the steep, ladder-like staircase only that morning. What a pathetic appeal, even to the sympathies of Jack, were those moans of half-conscious suffering.

"Dang the horse what did it!" said John Drake, as he gazed with an angry sympathy; "and dang the madam a-riding

the hoss—cuss her, a-riding over the
innocent—damn her!" So he made the
three steps of imprecation, looking all the
while upon Doll's drawn, yet pretty, oh so
pretty face.

" Thank you kindly, ma'am," he said,
going over to Mrs. James, and as he spoke
clumsily pulling his forelock; "it's right
good of you to stay i' the lass."

Mrs. James felt within her own soul that
it was certainly *not bad;* but, as is the
custom, she made light of the truly meri-
torious deed, and fussed noiselessly about
the mean room, making sundry preparations
for her own and Doll's comfort. Poor
Doll, with her shattered head and fractured
ribs, lay benumbed with pain, and stupefied
with ether, and deaf and blind to all
external influences.

" I was not able to tell Angela, as I had
intended doing," Bertie said, after they
had walked a few steps of their way home
in silence. He uttered the words with an
abruptness that was ejaculatory. He had
hoped that Clemence would question him;

but Clemence was too delicately proud a woman, and too fond a sister to do so.

"Have you not?" she replied quietly, then added, "I suppose that it was impossible to have anything like connected talk if the horse was gay, and Angela frightened."

"It was exactly so," he answered eagerly, coming nearer to her; "it was altogether out of the question. Angela was frightened out of all coherence or attention; but to-morrow it shall be got over." He set his teeth, and drew his eyebrows together, with the expression of a man preparing for an ordeal; for the poison of a woman's re-criminating words. Clemence expressed no doubt nor uncertainty of his doing as he said, even if she felt it.

"Pray take my arm," were his next words, a short pause having ensued; "you must be very tired."

"Thanks, no; I do not feel at all tired."

"Eyes right!" he cried half jestingly, half entreatingly, for she had turned her

head away, and was pensively looking
down at the sleeping daisies. The eyes
did not obey him; but she raised them,
and looked straight forward now, and he
could see the long lashes defined against
the faded primrose sky.

"What an odd thing love is!" he exclaimed impulsively; "mine for you was
not 'a love at first sight' weed. No,
Clemence, you sowed the seed in my
heart, and it grew slowly to be the deepest-
rooted and most tenacious of plants. It
was inadvertently sown, dear cousin; any
one more wanting in the malice prepense
of feminine wiles than you are, never
existed."

"You are not right in naming that gift of
pleasing 'malice prepense,'" she answered;
"it is a charming gift, of which its possessors
are often unconscious. Take my sister
Angela, for instance. Any one can see
the impression she produces upon every
living creature with whom she is thrown;
yet I know that she makes no sort of effort
to please."

"Angela is fascinating, but you are lovable," returned Bertie. "Clemence," he went on thoughtfully, "it is the fashion I know in fiction to represent the good young woman as having everything to fear from her wicked sister in the way of appropriating lovers; but I think that in real life the good sister wins it over the wicked. I say 'good' and 'wicked;' that needs qualification, of course. But I mean that the girl of pretty 'traits,' generally finds more earnest lovers at the last, than the girl of pretty features; the girl of warm heart and deep feeling, gains more enduring affection than she of deep intellect and shallow heart."

"I cannot agree with you," she rejoined; "when I think of the great enslavers who have driven men mad."

"Oh, the great enslavers had heart enough for one fellow," said Bertie; then the talk drifted into personalities as it will inevitably do, if one of two people is determined that it shall.

It was that time of the day, which is

sweet to the eye, as the echo of a clear musical strain is delightful to the ear. The sun had gone; but the after-glow was there. Many of the flowers were closing their petals; the daisies had closed theirs with a blush—but they had given the warm air an intenser perfume. It seemed to Bertie that Clemence must say one little kind, encouraging word to him now! An affection couched in sturdy Saxon words and demonstrated by liberal caresses, she would never give, he knew; but one little tender look; one responsive word?

No; Clemence gave neither: and her dignity to-night seemed to be an armed dignity. Bertie would have been assuaged could he have known that she was in part armed against herself. Clemence felt that unless she was loyal to her sister in deed, and in truth, at this time, she should never cease to reproach herself.

She was gentle; that she always was; and with gentleness, her cousin was obliged to be satisfied. A star, like a bright light held by a trembling hand, quivered in the empyrean. Clemence felt that if Angela had been there, she would have wished to it, for she was superstitious. Poor Angela! what never-to-be-gratified wish might she not have wished, Clemence thought sadly; and, although the evening was lovely enough to be a poet's theme, and although Bertie was with her, she was glad when the walk was over.

CHAPTER X.

" The wind is still, the stars are fled,
The melancholy moon is dead."

HEN they reached home they found dinner nearly over. Angela, apparently none the worse for her fright, was eating cherry-tart with no visible absence of appetite. A story of her own manufacture had greeted the ears of Miss Lawless, the squire, and Fox—also of Adrian, who had arrived shortly before dinner—therefore there was little for Clemence and Bertie to add, but to report the condition of the unfortunate child.

Angela turned to them as they entered,

and her lips got a trifle paler as she asked, " How is the child ?"

" She is very much hurt," answered Clemence, " but she is unconscious now, and, except for an occasional moan of pain, one would not think that she was suffering at all. We found Mr. Hurst there, and a good creature, a Mrs. James, wife of the saddler."

" But she will not *die ?*" interrupted Angela, for once laying a fervent stress upon one word.

" They think not ; oh, no—console yourself, Angela, they quite think not ; she is so young, and hardy, and full of animal strength ; she will pull through, never fear."

" All that I can say is, that it is a most unfortunate affair," remarked Miss Lawless.

Everybody at the table looked as if her non-ability to say more was a relief to them.

" Poor child,—it comes hard on you, very," said Mr. Lawless, with a compassionate glance at his fragile niece, who at that moment was looking as if she could lean her parian forehead upon the table, and faint, or die, with the utmost ease.

" Half the accidents from runaways that one hears of are caused by either children or dogs frightening the horses," said Adrian, decisively.

" But this child did not frighten Moonshine," replied Bertie, with equal decision ; " it was one of those cases where a little nerve would have made it all right. Angela pulled the curb rather more sharply than she was aware of, and the mare was bad-mannered enough to rear. I told Angela to drop the curb, but she did not understand—"

" You cruel fellow !" cried Angela, striking in. " After the agony of fright that I have suffered, to reproach me—to blame me when I only escaped with my life—"

" And limb," said Clemence, calmly.

" Heartless ! both of you," exclaimed Angela, with a choking sob. " Oh, I would not have believed it."

" I assure you," replied Bertie, with so

much feeling that any one could see that
Angela was mollified, " I was awfully sorry
for you, as I rode behind you, and watched
your hair shake down, and heard you
scream.   But, my dear child, never scream
again when a horse seems inclined to bolt.
And there was nothing in life to be frightened at ; come, now,—think—was there ?
Only to keep your saddle ; no very difficult
feat ; for a horse going at that speed always is smoother in its gait than when at
a slower pace.   I'm not a bit unfeeling ;
neither is Clemence.   You have my sincerest sympathy—if you feel that you re-
quire it !" And he laughed good-naturedly.
" Poor little girl !" he went on, with a com-
pression of his lips, " everything must be
done for her that can be done.   We must
send her broths, and jellies, and things of
that sort every day."

Mr. Lawless's face fell several degrees.
" We had better have doctor's orders for
soups and jellies before we send 'em," he
said irascibly.   " Nothing that the sun
shines on should be wasted."

" The jelly that the sun shines on would not be long in being wasted," Fox remarked with a boyish laugh. His father looked minaciously at him, and continued his dinner.

Strive as they might to bring other topics to the fore, that of the afternoon's catastrophe was sure to stray in like an unwanted poor relation. Angela winced at it, Bertie frowned, the corners of Clemence's mouth drooped, Mr. Lawless scowled, yet in it would persist in coming. Runaway horse ; knocked-down child ; would she recover? would she be disabled? how old was she? Why need so untoward an event have happened to the family of Lawless? (This last Miss Lawless's plaint.) They rang the changes on it, the ill-luck of it, and the pity of it, until Angela—all nerves—was on the point of fainting—at least so she frankly announced —and that unless the subject was tabooed, she should be obliged to leave the table and go to her room, she said.

So at last they made a leper of the topic,

and by their marked avoidance of it, or anything that might by chance lead up to it, Angela was satisfied.

Her nerves were not quite so unstrung that she could not, upon reaching the drawing-room, take up the long blue strip of lace-work that wound its slow length along, going at about the average of one inch a night.

Pale as Angela always was, to-night her pallor was terrible.   Adrian, going over to her, looked commiseratingly down upon her, an unwonted gentleness softening the fire of his dark eyes.

"You look just a little shattered by your fright," he said.

She leaned back in her chair, let the blue strip fall, and raised her blue eyes to his.

"Yes, I am a little shattered," she replied, repeating his own words, "and I feel strangely chilled; fingers of snow seem touching me; icy breaths seem to fan me. And I feel so dreamy; you look miles away from me."

" Do let me send for a glass of wine for you; you look very pale."

" I am always pale, you know," she replied, "and I won't have any wine, thanks. Do sit down. It tires me to see you standing, even though you do not shift from one leg to the other, which I hate to see a man do. And it tires me to look up at you."

Adrian seated himself as desired.

" I am horribly sorry for this poor little girl," said Angela, doing one intricate stitch in a leisurely manner.

" Oh, naturally ;—of course. But she must have been rather stupid, and not at all 'spry,' as the Yankees say,—not to have got out of your way, if you gave her time enough."

" Oh, a perfect owl, I do assure you," returned Angela, tranquilly. " I shouted to her ; I implored her to move. But she is pretty; oh, so pretty; I do hope that her face is not hurt;" and Angela shuddered, for she had a morbid horror of personal disfigurements. Yet she was the kind of woman who, in visiting Paris, would not have failed to seek the Morgue, and would have extracted from that bourne of exanimate horrors a shocking, yet genuine, satisfaction. Over it she could have her fill of shudders, could grow hysterically moved.

Adrian echoed her hope, and then a short pause fell between them, wherein Angela knit her delicate brows over the intricacies of her Spanish rose. Not so intricate was it but that she could steal a glance at her cousin and lover; her fervidly-loved Bertrand, who, seated beside Clemence, was talking to her with a strange air of absorption. Angela watched him with complacency, however, for to fear her sister would have made her suspect herself of approaching mental aberration. What? Bertie prefer sunshine to moonshine, prose to poetry, realism to ideality, girlish comeliness to Nixie loveliness, fact to fancy, human nature's plain "daily food" to the witch-like repast that she was always ready to spread? No, the thing was impossible!

She had sent Adrian across the room to fetch her a reel of thread, when the door was opened, and Henry North was ushered in, with a very faint suspicion of cigar-smoke about him.

" I thought that I might venture to stroll over," he said, apologetically ; " I believe we are not supposed to be on terms of ceremony together."

" Certainly not," answered Bertie ; " of course not."

Then Henry seated himself near Angela, and before long was entertained by her with a detailed account of the accident of the afternoon.

" Poor little girl !" he exclaimed with much compassion, as Angela paused.

" I am ' poor,' certainly, but I don't know that I can allow you to call me ' little girl,' " she returned, with languid coquetry, and a little smile.

" Oh, I did not mean *you*," he said, opening his eyes, rather. " You are all right, thanks be. I meant the poor little girl that you knocked over."

"I wish," said Angela with irritation, "that you would not talk of me as if I were a prize-fighter—poor little thing," she continued, with a dawning uneasy consciousness that he was weighing her in some balance of his own, and finding her wanting. "I am going to send over the very first thing to-morrow morning to know what I can do for her."

Henry North *was* weighing her, and he could not help but find her wanting in one of womanhood's most touching gifts—tenderness.

"I congratulate you on your own good luck," he said in a conventional tone. "You had a capital, quiet road, and a nice cool time of the day for a bolt, had you not?"

"You talk of it very much as Bertie does," she rejoined, with a defined sulkiness. "What would have been play to you, was something very like death to me."

"Oh, dear, no; impossible. Why you are looking uncommonly well to-night. So is your sister," glancing over at her ; " that expression of proud gentleness, like a beautiful wild creature mal apprivoisé, with which she is looking up at Bertie, is specially becoming to her, and so he seems to think, by Jove !"

" What astonishing discoveries you make in regard to my sister," exclaimed Angela, while a faint ray of colour stole into her face.

" I don't think what I have just said can be called an astonishing discovery," he replied.

Angela regarded her cousin and her sister earnestly for a moment, and then said emphatically, " I am quite willing for my Bertie to approve of my sister."

" So ?" he breathed out. " That possessive pronoun, as you pronounce it, holds a world of meaning."

" I intend it to do so," she rejoined, glancing proudly over at Bertie's handsome face. " I do not care to hide as a secret what I am contented that all the world should know."

Although he was not in love with her, he yet could not take this revelation with indifference, and after murmuring, "Most fortunate of fellows!" drew Angela's gaudy work-basket towards him, and began turning over its contents, his eyes following his hands, so that he need not look her in the face. Proud and pleased was she at this proof of her might.

Presently he began to be amused at the varied stores of that feminine receptacle on his knees. Here was a little flat pincushion cut out of violet silk, and painted to represent a pansy. He felt that he should like to appropriate it; it was so pretty, so small, and so flat.

"Bertie admires that," observed Angela. "I am going to give it him."

"Ha!" said Henry, and continued his search. He found a shark's tooth mounted in gold now, and a pink satin bag next, filled with poudre d'iris. A little thimble surrounded by turquoises, evidently kept for holiday occasions, for she had a plain one on her finger now. A pair of small, gilded scissors; a little mother-of-pearl box containing a flower that had long ago departed this life.

" I suppose Bertie once wore that in his coat ?" he said, interrogatively. She blushed very deeply, and was significantly silent. He caught a sigh half way breathed, and changed it into a little laugh. Why should he care, he thought, whether or not this girl, whose heart was as cold as a toad embedded in a rock, sentimentally cherished a flower which her betrothed had once worn ? He went on ransacking the basket. Here was a little blood-stone seal with her initials A. A. L. upon it. She never used it. In these days of "chiffres," who does use seals ?

"What does the second A stand for ?" he asked.

"Amy; I am Angela Amy; Clemence is Clemence Frances. Bertie thinks Amy prettier than Angela ; I tell him to adopt the name of Amy for me, if he likes, and let it be used by him alone."

Henry dropped the seal suddenly back

again, and it fell clinking among the reels,
and stilettoes, and needle-cases.

"I determined that I would call him
Bertrand," Angela continued. "I dislike
diminutives so much for men; but, as you
see, I have drifted into Bertie. I called
him Bertrand once, I think, and once only.
Then Bertie is a name of itself you know,
which betters matters. But Adrian I do
call Adrian, not Adie, a most ignominious
appellation, and about as suitable to him
as 'Fido' to the lady's hippopotamus in
that absurd picture that came out in 'Punch'
ages ago. I am angry just at this moment
with both Bertie and Clemence; they made
so light of my being run away with. Bertie
I shall forgive to-night; he will make me
do it, I know; but Clemence I shall insist
upon having a silent feud with until to-
morrow; then I shall kiss and be friends,
for I want her to make me a Dolly Varden
cap; and it's inconvenient to ask a favour
of a person with whom you are having a
silent feud, isn't it?"

"I dare say. I never had one, however."

" No ? Not with Bertie in other days ?"

" Oh, dear, no. Bertie is the last person with whom it would be possible to have one, as you have just admitted. You say that he will make you forgive him to-night. I know what that means."

" What ?"

" Oh, well, we'll call it moral suasion."

At this point, what had been a tête-à-tête between them, was broken in upon by Adrian, and soon Miss Lawless as well included herself in the conversation. At half-past ten the Lawless establishment overstepped the bounds of stinginess to the degree of providing rather warm claret cup, which young North was chary of imbibing, and presently rising up, made his farewells, not having spent quite as agreeable an evening as he had anticipated doing.

CHAPTER XI

"ANGELA," said Clemence, upon reaching their room that night, "my heart aches."

"Does it? poor thing! I am sorry that you cannot have it painlessly extracted like a tooth."

"It aches," Clemence went on, disregarding her sister's facetiousness, "to see you so apparently unfeeling—*apparently*—I am sure that in your heart you are as sorry as possible for that poor little girl—little Dorothy Drake——"

"Oh, is that her name? Yes, of course I am sorry. Horribly sorry. What can I do for her? But don't tell me to-night. I am so tired and sleepy, and I have such a crawley, creepy feeling all down my back

I think I've heard that it was a precursor of fever; but *you* would not care; you have been abominably unfeeling about me, your only sister. I think that you would have been rather entertained if I had been brought home this afternoon on a shutter."

" Oh, Angela, for shame! How——"

" I have told you once, Clemence, that I don't feel equal to talking, and it is cruel of you to persist. How can you look at such a pathetic-looking thing as I see in the glass, and not attend to what it says?"

" Only say good-night to me, and I won't bother you any more," answered Clemence, humbly; "and tell me that you know I give you all my best sympathy and all my best love."

"Good-night," responded Angela amiably, touched by her sister's tender tone; " I know that you're fond of me, and are good to me, and are glad that I am safe. There, now you are contented, I am sure. Poor Henry North," she went on suddenly, "he was a portrait of a collapsed gentleman when I told him about Bertie."

"What did you tell him about Bertie?"

"That is not an intelligent question, Clemence. What was I likely to tell him, but that I was engaged to Bertie? Of course I did not say so in just those unburnished words, but it amounted to the same thing; he understands how it is, and by this time I suppose his friend, his mother, does as well."

"Oh, Angela! premature on your part."

"You certainly can be a most detestable creature when you choose, Clemence. Between Bertie and me must a declaration concise and arid as an act of Parliament be made and accepted. Why, that would rob me of half my pleasure; and Bertie, with his keen and quick insight into my character, knows precisely how to deal with me. However, to-morrow he will probably insist upon saying something definite, I am afraid (I wish he would leave affairs in this most halcyon and unarranged state a little longer); but he announced that he must talk to me to-morrow morning, as soon after breakfast as possible, and he

made the request with the solemnity
of an Iroquois proposing to unbury the
hatchet. It is the step in life, of course,
and the only step. Birth and death can't
be called steps. In the one case we are
shuffled into life without our leave, and in
the other we are shuffled out of it. But
the selection of a wife is a very different
thing——"

"I believe I am a coward!" interrupted
Clemence violently, and flinging herself
down on the rug beside her bed, she buried
her face in the pillow.

"I have been afraid that it was hard for
you to wish me joy," answered Angela,
easily. "It is a sad pity that you should
have been——but don't let us put what we
mean into words. You must learn to
think of him as a brother, Clemence; it is
very easy to tutor one's self into these
things; and I will manage to keep him
apart from you, after, after—at first I
mean. Oh, don't howl and cry like that,
it is so unlike you."

"Bertie," began Clemence, when Angela held up her hand, and peremptorily bade her stop. "No more talking to-night, I don't want to hear what you have to say, and I *will not* look like the ghost of my great-grandmother to-morrow."

And with these good-night words, Miss Angela Lawless extinguished the candle, and hiding the match-box under her pillow, left her partially-dressed sister on the floor in the dark.

Long after Angela was asleep Clemence sat there. She was a moral coward, she told herself. A very loving one, but a coward all the same. And was a man worth loving, who, by his thoughtlessness and sentimentality, would cause two hearts to ache grievously ? "Ah," came the answer, " if only those worth loving were loved, the boy-god might lay aside his quiver and bow, and bury his arrows for ever." A conflict went on within her, down on the rug in the dark, and listening to her sister's long respirations.

To allow Angela to persist in a fatal mistake like this, and make no revelation to her, was a kind of barbarity. Yet should not the revelation come from Bertie? Yes; it was all in his hands. But was not she a poor faltering fool, to permit her sister to go to the man she fancied was her lover, unprepared, when she might be in a measure prepared? And she saw distinctly, that to Angela, imprisoned in self as she was, and proud with the pride of intense vanity, what she would be called upon to undergo, to-morrow, would be little short of torture. To be supplanted by herself—Clemence—there would be the excruciation to Angela, who had ever ranked her sister so low!

Impulsively Clemence got upon her feet, and groped her way towards her sister's bed. The clock on the landing struck one, sonorously; then many smaller clocks tinkled one from different parts of the house. The window stood wide open, and in the distance she heard the little fox-terrier howling for his master. And she could hear the shrubs and trees rustling and murmuring out in the dark, starless night. A bird twittered feebly, as if it was talking in its sleep. She touched her sister caressingly on the arm. Angela stirred.

" Angela," said Clemence.

" What do you want ?" answered Angela awaking with a start. " You know how I hate you when you come and wake me out of sound sleep like this. What is it ?"

" I want to speak to you ; I must speak to you."

" Oh, heavens ! she wakes me out of a deep first sleep, after a day spent in being run away with by a horse, and then says *'she wants to speak to me.'* You shan't," with a snarl, " I won't listen to you ; the next thing will be, that you will come and wake me up to tell me that I am asleep ! Be off with you."

"Oh, do attend to me ; it is about Bertie that I want to speak."

" Ah, that is 'a trap,' not to catch a ' sunbeam,' but a sleepy listener. I will not listen even to anything about him. Get to bed, do."

" Angela, he is going to say something

to you to-morrow, that you will *hate* to
hear."

" The English of which is that he is
going to give me a jealous scolding about
Henry North. Why need you meddle in
my affairs ? Take your hand off my arm."

" No, no, he will do nothing of the sort,"
cried Clemence in despair of making her
sister understand her ; " oh, Angela, you
are falling asleep ! You will not then
listen, when what I want to say is of vital
interest and importance to you."

Without replying, Angela produced the
match-box from under her pillow, lighted
the candle beside her bed, and taking her
sister's face ungently between both hands
stared into it.

" There is no moon to-night ? no ; and
I never heard of anybody being star-
struck ; besides, there are not any stars.
Now what is the matter with you,
Clemence ? And you are crying again !
Here is a singular development ; tears,
sleeplessness, dramatic fervour, jealousy,
addled innuendoes——and you so common-

place! Have you an inkling of what is the matter with you? If you have, I should like to be told in two words, and then I should wish to get inside the ivory gates again. I shall count ten, and then put the candle out; the light disturbs me very much, and you can manage perfectly well in the dark; *I* could. Come." And Angela grasped the candle firmly in one hand, and the extinguisher in the other, having already replaced the match-box under her pillow.

"I cannot, when you are in so mocking, and uncomfortable, and inattentive a frame of mind," returned Clemence, losing her temper, and walking away. "I had to screw myself up to the proper pitch of courage to wake you, I assure you; and I would rather have been beaten, than say what I thought it my duty to say."

"Bah! Aunt Maria!" said Angela slightingly, and, without going through the proposed ceremony of counting ten, extinguished the candle, very pleased to snub Clemence by not betraying the faintest curiosity about what she had to divulge.

CHAPTER XII.

NGELA'S adornment of her fair person was careful and prolonged the next morning, and its result highly satisfactory to her when she drew off and surveyed herself in the glass. A Dolly Varden cap, which Clemence had made for her, surmounted her fine pale hair; there were lavender bows, matching its ribbons, at her throat and waist; and she wore a captivating little black fichu. Finally, she ran downstairs, and on her way snatched a white climbing rose, which nodded good-morning to her through the open window of the landing. Adjusting it coquettishly, she considered

VOL. I.   16

herself then complete, and, entering the deserted breakfast-room (she was invariably the last), rang for hot tea and rolls, and made a sustaining repast.

She had arranged to meet Bertie at a certain spot ; and to this trysting-place she presently betook herself, singing his name over and over as she went.

At the side of the house a wide walk sloped away, clean, yellow, and smooth, and lost itself among the shrubbery. Half way, it was broken by a flight of three stone steps, and upon each side of the highest step stood a stone urn, filled now with salmon-coloured geraniums. It was by these urns that she had agreed to meet her cousin, and there he waited, leaning against one of them, and smoking.

He threw his cigar away as she tripped towards him, singing and smiling. She held out both hands to him, but he only took one, and that one he held loosely for a second, and then let it go. He saw the brilliancy of vexation come into her eyes, and she said petulantly—

"And now what is it that you are so eager to say to me? Is it something nice? or are you going to be foolish and jealous enough to scold me again about Henry North?"

"I am neither going to do one thing nor the other," he replied, gravely; "not that I am aware of ever having '*scolded*' you about Henry North. No, Angela, no; I am going to try and do what is right, according to my light, and I have nerved myself to endure your keen reproaches, and the reproaches of my own conscience, still more keen.

"Angela, how do you think I love you? What did your charm and bewitchment lead me into saying the day before yesterday? I love you as the sweetest, most fascinating of cousins—sisters; but I should be a coward to allow you to go on thinking that I prize you beyond any creature that the world holds. They were bungling half-truths that I said to you; I did not—not —express myself aright; and the consciousness of that has been driving me half mad

16—2

since I said them. Seeing that you were misunderstanding me, for one mad moment I determined to be what you supposed me to be, and never to make any confession of this sort to you. Forgive me!—you are too charming, and too powerful in your fascination and beauty not to be merciful; pray be so!

"Angela, you love your sister?" he went on with a startling abruptness, longing to make an end of the detestable scene.

"You do!" she answered in an icy voice. "I see it all now. Spare yourself and me further details of your miserable vacillation, you despicable pendulum! I am sorry that my name is your name. You bungler!—to drag me out here that you might suffocate me with that clumsy patchwork of words!"

She sank down upon the highest step, leaning her head back against the urn; and he watched her lovely face grow ashy, while a fine line like a white cord became defined along the outline of her upper lip.

"Angela! Angela!" he cried, terrified.

Then a crimson streak flamed into her left cheek, and she burst into a torrent of tears.

"I am sorry that I ever saw you," she said, in an altered voice. "Oh! I would rather that you had killed me than brought me so low as this! Oh, Bertie! Bertie! I want my old pride to scorn you with, but it is gone from me! I want my bitter tongue to punish you with, but it will not speak for me! I want my old, fiery temper that a word kindled into a flame, but it fails me. Clemence has been playing a Judas' part towards me—the meek, sly robber! Yes, a Judas' part towards me; for you loved her long ago, did you not? And she knew it. She has been triumphant in her heart, knowing me to be the vanquished one—woe to me!—and deceiving me with a placid face! I know now why I caught her last evening staring at me like an owl in the sunshine :—she was regarding me as a curious thing in blights; the possessor of a ruinous little spot that *she* saw, but that I was unconscious of. You have acted a cruel part towards me ; but I do not feel half as hardly towards you as I do towards *her*."

"That is not the way to speak," said Bertie, agitated to the point of only being able to utter the most unsuitable commonplaces. "I have not intended, I assure you, to act a cruel part towards you. I have always prized you as a most charming companion and cousin. But I grew to know Clemence so well, in the rides we have taken together ; and from learning to know her, I learnt to love her.

"She has neither been sly nor deceptive —Clemence is incapable of being either—for I have said nothing to her until last night. She knows that she is not half so pretty and charming as you are ; no one could be more humble as to her own opinion of herself than she is. You will get over—this —I believe."

He tried not to meet her eyes as he spoke, but they followed his with an insistence that drew his own unwillingly to meet them. They were wobegone, and desti-

tute of one ray of hope. They were dry
and bright, yet they betrayed more misery
than is betokened by unquenchable tears.

" Tell me more of this carefully conducted love-affair of yours," she said, in a
thin, hard voice.

He was about to refuse, when she leaned
forward, saying vehemently :—

" But I insist ; I *will* hear. I am in a
fever of curiosity. Come, when did you
first make up your mind to the fact that
your soul and Clemence's descended from
Heaven a pair ?"

" I will not answer," he replied, grudg-
ingly ; " you are making a fool of me."

" Making a fool of you !" she repeated ;
"and what have you made of me ? Am
I not spirited to sit here, with my tears all
wiped away, and be able to question you
like this ?"

" It is because you don't care two straws
about me," answered he, in a tone of profound thankfulness, that was heart-rending
to his listener.

" Oh, you mistake ; I love you dearly—

as a cousin. I think I mistook my feeling in regard to you—oh——" she cried, breaking down utterly, "that this should be *I!* Hush—do not speak! It will be needless brutality to attempt further extenuation or blame of yourself. I understand quite, quite well how it was—*now.* I think I will go in. How glaring the sun is; how it beats down on this yellow sand——"

"You forgive me?" Bertie interrupted; "you do not care? Come, admit that you do not."

"That is a cowardly question," she replied, speaking through her clenched teeth. "How is it that you can have such brave, frank eyes, such firm and honest features, be so tall and strong, and yet be so mean, so cowardly, and so cruel?"

"I suppose I must be dumb," he said, in a stifled voice.

"I suppose you must be," she repeated, "for you can have nothing really in self-defence to say."

She turned to go.

"Stop," he said, detaining her; "before you go, say something to soften the insult and reproach of those words of yours to me. They rankle and burn like red-hot arrows. To be called *coward* is that which a man's whole nature revolts against."

" Men lose no prestige, nor no woman's love, because they are *moral* cowards," said Angela, with a piteous tenderness in her voice, and in her trembling smile, as she looked at him, " and that is all I accused you of being."

" All !" he echoed, "*all !*"

" Yes, all. Did you not just tell me that you were on the point of gliding into a position that was false as false could be ? I know what it was that held you back ; the thought of Clemence. And the thought of Clemence, whom you love, and whom you would lose, else, has fortified you to-day in saying what you have said. I grow sick and faint when I think of how I have spoken to her of *you*, and she, the dumb adder, to hear me out without contradiction. She, my sister, who I fancied loved me more than any one in the world."

"She left it for me to say," he murmured.

A refreshing thought flashed through Angela's mind, that perhaps Clemence did not feel sure of her lover! While the comfort of it was still with her, it were best to go, she thought.

"Good-bye, Bertie——" she stopped abruptly, and walked rapidly away into the house.

Bertie, folding his arms upon the rim of the urn, bowed his head upon them, and the luxuriance of the pink flowers hid his quivering mouth and miserable eyes.

Many minutes he stood there, overwhelmed with intense annoyance and self-reproach, then, turning off from the path, he walked away to where a magnolia in full flower spread its broad leaves, and flinging himself down in their shade, drew his hat over his face, and tried to banish from his mind that late disagreeable scene; but mental repetitions of it were all that

the thinking power could conjure. The
sweep of a woman's gown over the bright,
dry grass, roused him, and it was with an
almost childish delight, and an intense
sense of relief that he recognized Clemence, with an unusually perturbed face,
advancing towards him.

" Is it over ?" she asked, anxiously, sink-
ing down on the grass beside him.

" Yes ; it is over," he answered, shortly.
" I wish you could see her before we go
to Barport ; and, Clemence, never ask me
to tell you any of the particulars of this
most trying scene that I have just had with
your sister."

" I will not," said Clemence, in hearty
assent. Then she rose up and returned to
the house. Bertie was in no mood for
talking, she saw, and it did not surprise
her.

At the door of her own room she en-
countered her sister face to face, who, with
hat, veil, and parasol, seemed to be starting
for a walk. Moreover, she had a sketch ·
book under her arm.

"Angela," faltered Clemence, "you are not angry with me, are you?"

"Angry? No," replied Angela, lifting her veil, and fixing her burning blue eyes upon her sister. "Angry! that is not the word. Clemence, if I were to bite you at this moment, you would have some sort of 'phobia."

Clemence was intensely relieved to hear a speech so like Angela's own whimsical self, and tried to catch her sister in her arms and kiss her. But Angela, eluding her, stepped aside, and descended the stairs. She laughed faintly as she went— a sound sweet to Clemence's ears—but there was Satanism in her face.

She went out of the house, and strayed through the park like a lost dog, finally creeping through the wire railing of a thickly-grown plantation. Here, amongst the murmuring pines and the hemlocks, and the straight smooth beauty of superb fern-leaved beeches, she was secluded, quiet, and estranged from all human beings but her dangerous self.

She did not cast herself down upon the mossy ground, or mutter daft-sounding ejaculations, or, sobbing, wind her fingers in her soft fair hair. No; seating herself decorously as if eyes were upon her, at the foot of a gloomy and sighing cedar, mechanically she placed her sketch-book on her knees, and, opening it, dragged her pencil across and across the page, with such force that it pricked and tore the strong elephant paper. Then she sat stolidly staring at the jet black marks, until her eyes ached and burned with the unwinking fixedness of their gaze. She closed the lids for an instant, and when she opened them, she took in, for the first time, that the leafy scene by which she was environed was lovely, and that the sky was summer's own tranquil blue, and the sunshine topaz, and the birds' voices ear-caressing, as they poured forth joyous epithalamium and jubilate.

"This sweeps and garnishes my soul," she muttered to herself, with a frown, and gazing up to where

"Heavily were drifting
White clouds to the shore of blue, away."

There were no graceful and pleasing fancies now, nestling at her heart. Into it, and into her garnished soul, stepped dangerous usurpers, a powerful pack, of whom reckless endeavour and costly sin might be born. Fancies, clear and vivid as Dutch pictures, occupied her mind. She did not scruple to admit them; they were welcome. Vindictive and retaliative though they were, she yet hugged them to her, as a mother her deformed child.

The breezy, golden forenoon was fast becoming languid, airless, burning; the birds were almost still; the leaves had altogether ceased to murmur; and the downy clouds had sailed away to their haven on the edge of the horizon, when Angela bethought herself of such things as home and luncheon; and marking in her mind the hours spent amongst those shadowy trees as the bitterest, the most nauseous of her life, she rose to her feet, took her sketch-book, and began to loiter

homewards, over the velvet knolls, and the
long strips of ardent sunshine, and the
ragged bits of shade, through the shrub-
beries, full of flowers as a London ball¬
room of women, and into the house.

"Let me see your sketch," said Clemence,
trying to speak easily, as Angela sank down
into a chair near her. (There was no one
at the table but the three women.) Angela,
with her indescribable smile, that seemed
always to press the circulation from out
her lips and turn them white, opened the
book, and in silence displayed to her sister
the jagged and unmeaning-looking black
scratches that she had made. Unmeaning!
There was the meaning of a heart full of
repressed fury and torment in them.

" Nonsense !" said Clemence, looking
first at them, and then at her sister, with a
forced smile and a look of frightened per-
plexity in her eyes. "Is this really all
that you have done in all these hours ?"

" This is all," Angela replied, with an
iced ferocity of manner under which Clemence shrank.

"I have been spending the morning with Doll," she said, trying to make a little conversation. "She is a shade better, already."

"Is she?" Angela repeated. "Aunt Maria, have you praised Clemence for going? I hope so; for she considers herself a consummate Samaritan, you may be sure. Let us glorify her to her face, or she will think us the most unappreciative of sinners."

Miss Lawless eyed her younger niece with the expression of a dog-fish surprised, and made answer that she had told Clemence "that it was a good sort of thing in her to do."

"Oh! but that won't satisfy her," said Angela, rancorously; "I mean to praise her *ad nauseam*—she expects it."

"You shall do nothing of the sort," replied Clemence, with a quiet dignity, and rising from the table. "I cannot think why you have chosen to talk in so absurd a strain. Will you be less crooked after lunch, think you? And will you come out under the rose-trellis for a short time, and let me have a word with you ?"

" No," returned Angela, in a tone of arduously repressed ire.

" *Please* do ?"

" No," repeated Angela, in the same tone as before.

Clemence, being anything but supermundane, could not find words wherewith to coax and urge her. Therefore, taking refuge in silence the golden, she left the room, and, getting her work, went out under the roses with it ; thus leaving Angela the undisputed possession of her room, which Angela availed herself of, retiring thither, and, in lonely abjectness, spending the long hours of the breathless June afternoon. Now and then the lightest murmur of voices came to her from the rose-walk, and she knew, she *felt*, that they belonged to her sister and Bertie, who, in the enjoyment of the first sweet and novel hours of betrothal—unembittered, she feared, by any thought of her—were talking together amongst the tangled glow of the roses,

that crept over the trellis above their heads
and drooped crimson, and pale pink, and
pure white—all scented—in the airless sunshine.   And she had never suspected! had
never seen danger to Bertie in those long,
undisturbed rides—with Clemence!   Danger, and Clemence!—the very combination
of the two words seemed gallingly ludicrous
to her.

Clemence! with her gray eyes that
never did anything but *see*, and look straight
forward, or perhaps droop quietly like a
nun's telling her beads.   Clemence, who
had no tricks or graces of manner, no
coquetries of gesture, no witcheries of
voice, or speech, or smile—who was only a
large, sensible, commonplace young woman,
with a cheerful temperament, a warm heart,
a total want of capriciousness and whimsicality, no beauty to speak of, and only the
grace that springs from fundamental energy,
and thoroughly strong health.

Angela twisted herself from side to side
of her little Arabian bed, and bit her pale
lips, and lost herself in contemptuous won-

der, and intense self-commiseration.   She
to be slighted for Clemence!   She to make
an idiot of herself!   It was unbearable!

Out among the roses the affianced ones
made each other happy with acknowledged
mutual love.   Clemence sewed on another
Dolly Varden cap for her sister, and Bertie
smoked a cheroot, mild-flavoured as they
usually are, and not in the least obnoxious
to either Clemence or the roses.

CHAPTER XII.

"Tanto gentile, e tanto onesta pare
Da donna mia quand' ella altrui saluta
Che ogni lingua divien, tremando muta
E gli occhi non ardiscon di guardare."

TO occupy the room with one towards whom we cherish jealousy, rancour, and animosity, is a dismal thing to do; and so Angela found it that night, and determined it should be the last. She would petition for a room to herself on the morrow, she promised herself.

Poor Clemence! she would rather have had from her sister a storm of abuse, a string of invectives, a downpour of reproaches, than the chill and ugly silence that Angela obstinately maintained—Angela, who was ordinarily so voluble.

It was a wretched night for the younger sister, and a sad one for the elder. Both were glad when, the candle being extinguished, there was no further occasion for timid, half-questioning, half-entreating words on the one part, and frozen, monosyllabic responses on the other.

That night was the last, until their lives ended, that they occupied the same room. For Angela on the following day moved to a room on the other side the house, and Clemence was left to herself.

And the cousins were affianced, and lived the full life of mutual love and trust.

Side by side with their lives, Angela's "crept on a broken wing." Like a wounded wild creature, she sought nothing half so much as the loneliness of lonely places, where the only sounds to be heard were the sounds of insentient nature,—for hers was the sort of suffering that must be as carefully hidden as if it were a sin.

Now and then the dull pain of disappointment and thwarted love was changed to the keener one of lacerated pride—

lacerated by the most conventional of words, uttered in the most conventional of manners.

"Oh! so it is your sister who is engaged to Mr. Bertie Lawless?" cried Miss De Manley in the middle of a formal visit; "odd, the garbled way in which things reach one. Why, we heard that it was *you* who were engaged to your cousin ; and not only we heard it, but a lot of other people." (Of course the "lot" should have been submitted to subtraction.)

Angela, pale as "snow on herbless peaks" before, flushed that painful sudden vivid flush which tells of a blow, or a sting, or a wound received, yet concealed.

"Odd, indeed," she said, with a little shrug of the shoulders. But Miss De Manley thought the blush more worthy of note than the reply, the cool tone, and the careless shrug.

"Angela!" said Clemence to her sister, later on that same day, when the two happened to be for a moment left alone together, "is this to go on for ever? Do you intend never to be the same again to me—my own sister, towards whom Providence has assigned me a hard part?"

"Providence," echoed Angela, with scorn.

"What else? Surely I would not have selected it. But, Angela, I could not give the man I loved, and who loved me, to my sister, even if I had chosen. I could have refused him—yes; but it would have been anything but a praiseworthy act. And how could it have had any good result? No, I have done right; I firmly believe I have."

"It must be a grateful feeling to be so self-satisfied," replied Angela, who had listened with scorn to a self-vindication so commonplace. "Take care that Bertie does not get to be a lover only at the point of the bayonet."

Clemence visibly winced; she did fear her sister's power, although she trusted Bertie as completely as she trusted herself.

Her nature was so dissimilar from her sister's, that she could not understand the havoc worked in Angela's by the mortification and disappointment that had overtaken her. For herself, she could never have fallen her own victim as Angela had done, and even the prescience which warm love gives failed to make her quite comprehend. Often she tried to sound her sister as to the depth and permanence of that regret and humiliation which she knew her to have endured. But Angela seemed to have crystallized herself. Her words were few and frozen to her sister; her manner icy; her answers curt and misleading. Clemence, baffled, ceased attempting to probe her, and, sheltering herself within her requited love, watched Angela still with anxious sisterly eyes, but forebore to subject herself to the chilling repulses that Angela was such a proficient in giving. As for making her the recipient of those confidences that will outflow from the fulness of a happy heart, that could never have come to pass, even if Angela's heart had laid no claim on her sister's lover; for Angela was not receptive, and would have been sure to subtly give her sister to understand that

her confidences were " commonplace," and
that she was more ready to give sneers
than sympathy. Yet Angela herself had
not been self-sufficing. She had demanded
in her short lifetime much sympathy from
her sister, and Clemence had given it un-
sparingly. Sympathy, and admiration, and
almost maternal tenderness and self-sacri-
fice. Angela was unconscious that she
was receiving priceless spiritual gifts from
her sister, and certainly made no return in
kind.

To that young life that was battling with
the foe, Suffering, Clemence gave sympathy
warm and deep ; and when the languid
consciousness of convalescence replaced the
fevered lapse of mental perception, was
thanked for it. Day after day she drove,
or walked, or rode into Barport, and took
her place for a watch of hours beside Dorothy Drake's bedside. She grew to know
every line of the pretty child face, pinched
now, and crimson—every motion of the
arms, every line of the fingers and hands.
A sense of proprietorship stole over her,

as it will over every watcher of an ill, and helpless, and suffering fellow-creature, regardless of age, or sex, or condition of life.

The day when Doll fixed faint languid eyes upon her, and said "Who are you, miss?" was a very happy one to Clemence, and, stooping over, she kissed the blue-veined temple lightly, replying, " I am Miss Lawless, Doll." From the utter passivity of weakness, Doll soon stole into the fuller life of regained strength and self-wonder, and awakened recollection. It was a strange, yet pleasant experience, to lie in the old room, tidy and habitable-looking now—thanks to Mrs. James and Clemence —and be fed by white, gentle hands, that touched her as tenderly as if she had been a wounded bird; to hear that agreeable tinkle of a gold chatelaine with its wonderful collection of trifles hanging on it, close to her ear; to be sensible of a vague perfume that shook itself from the lace encircling Clemence's round, violet-veined wrists, and from her ribbons, and the handkerchief in her pocket. And looking up (if she felt the strength for such exertion) to see a face that seemed to her half divine, with its stamp of gentle womanhood, and its grace of pity, and its beauty of soul, and life, and heart. Doll was conscious of an elevated tranquillity when the tall lady, with her proudly-poised head and assured movements, came into the room, and, bending over her, asked her a heart-felt question as to herself.

"Better, thank you, ma'am," was Doll's invariable reply. It seemed to her a point of honour to be "better," after all the kindness and care that had been lavished on her, and her grateful heart would allow her lips to frame no other answer. Doll felt translated in those languid days, when her young strength was mustering, and the half-severed ends of her life were knitting themselves together again.

Although even more ignorant than the typical rustic, she was not dull, or slow ; and as her strength returned to her, her pertinent childish questions aroused in Clemence a desire to free her clear young intellect, in a measure at least, from the fog of illiterateness. When Doll was well enough to crawl about like a fly in the March sunshine, Clemence still went on with her daily visits; and now she brought books —books usually where learning was taught pictorially, for though a great girl of fourteen, Doll's instruction was obliged to be such as would be given to a child of six. Clemence found her very educable. Her bright brown colt's eyes, which before her illness had shown no docility, nor much comprehension of anything save the most animal and sordid details of life, now began to absorb from Clemence's teaching and companionship, a most human beauty of intelligence and awakened perception. It seemed to Clemence that a more re-paying and agreeable task was never undertaken than this nursing and teaching Doll. The sense of proprietorship deepened, and pride in her protégée sprang up in her heart. For Nature had made Doll excessively pretty, and Clemence and books were making her quite beautiful, although she was at the proverbially ugly age of girlhood. Clemence had a roseate plan in her mind for translating Doll to Creyke, after her own marriage, and of polishing and educating her to a degree that should fit her to be a governess of children. *Whose* children, Clemence did not, to herself, of course, particularize.

Occasionally, in the morning, Bertie would make his appearance at Drake's cottage. Upon a certain Thursday he did so, and a more charming picture than that which met his eye cannot be imagined. A casement with greenish glass panes of the smallest, thrown wide open, and straggling tendrils of woodbine trembling on the edges. Clemence seated in an old wooden chair, with the back so preposterously rounded, that it was fitted to be a spoiler of shoulders, with an open book upon her knees, and at her feet, half leaning against her, with a mingling of shyness and confidence, Doll, in a new print gown, sprinkled thickly with rose-buds. Then there were to be heard distinctly the rush

of the mill-stream, the whirr of the great
wheel, the happy notes of sun-warmed
birds, busy at bird-work amongst the trees
outside.   Bertie entered, and seated himself on the window-ledge close to the pair.
The lesson went on, only interrupted by a
smile from Clemence, and a shy "good-
day, sir," from Doll.

He waited, listening to the lesson, until
Clemence closed the book, saying, "Very
good, Doll; you improve."

"Very good, Doll," he repeated, looking
kindly at the child; "I could not have
done better, myself, even with Miss Lawless to teach me."

Doll laughed a little, displaying dimples,
and very strong little square teeth, while
she screwed herself backward behind
Clemence, with all her old rusticity.

"You have a good memory, have not
you, Doll?" said Clemence, "and we don't
know, really, how good it is yet, for you
are not strong enough to be taught half as
much as you are able to learn."

"Oh, I am very well," replied Doll,

stoutly, but with a nervous sense of de-
siring to hide her tell-tale, thin, blue-
veined hands.

"Well," said Clemence, glancing at
them, "but not quite strong yet. Soon you
will be, you know, very soon. You are
able to walk a little out in the open air
already, are you not?"

"Yes," answered Doll; "yesterday I
walked a bit after father came home. He
helped me. My knees didn't feel like *my*
knees, they shook so. Dad, he says it's
alwus the way, the time you've been sick
like to I ha' been, and are getting well
again."

"But your head feels all right?" inquired
Bertie, lifting the hair from her forehead,
and exposing the large scar at the roots,
perilously near the temple.

"Oh, my head feels right," returned
Doll, "ever so right. My hearin's better
than ever it was, I think. I can hear the
osiers saying 'sh, sh,' to each other, the
last thing at night, beyant the splash of the
brook."

"I love the sound," said Clemence, closing her eyes for a moment to listen. "I love that sound of the water as it rushes over the dam, and then comes gurgling down past the cottage, between the willows and under the causeway. Don't you love the sound, Doll?"

It had never occurred to Doll before to love a sound; now, however, since it seemed that it was practicable to do so she decided that she did love it, and said so.

"When you grow to be a woman, Doll, you will dream of it, and even remember it quite well when you are awake. I dare say it was rushing and babbling on just in this way when you were born, and, perhaps, told the sea, as it rushed into it, that a new little pair of ears had come to listen to it. You were born in this cottage, were you not, Doll?"

"Yes," said Doll, "and mother she died the night."

"Poor mother!" said Clemence, in an accent of exquisite tenderness.

The tears rushed to Doll's eyes. Most

unexpected visitors were they. To cry
for the mother who had died at her birth,
would have seemed to her before like crying because she had lost her own shadow.
But there was that in Clemence's tone
which made the tears start suddenly.
Mother!—word so lovable. Poor mother
—of whose face she had not even the ghost
of a memory. Mother would doubtless
have been, living, a hard-worked drab,
with a worn visage, and horny hands, and
probably a very sharp voice ; but she would
have belonged to Doll, and Doll to her ;
and perhaps for her daughter would have
kept a certain tender tone, and an expression not for every-day use. A mother in
the land of shadows cannot be so lovable
to any young rustic, as the drudging help-
meet of the tiller of the soil, who calls her
"hussy," and gives her a shake here, and
a box on the ears there, and who exercises
a rough, but effectual supervision over her,
yet is to be found hard at work, always
ready to pause that she may tie up a bruised
head, or a cut hand, scolding vigorously

meanwhile, and using hasty words, but with fingers that touch tenderly, nevertheless.

Some such thought as this passed through Clemence's mind, and it occurred to her to try to endue the dead mother with a certain reality, which Doll might cling to, in her thoughts during those lonely hours when her father was at work.

"Who knows, Doll," she said with a smile, "your mother's eyes may be often, often on you as you wander over the fields, or sit at home waiting for your father to come? Perhaps she has been grieving over the pain that you have been obliged to suffer, and is very happy now to see you growing so well and strong again. Perhaps when you have said something kind or nice to your father, she has whispered to you to say it; who knows?"

"Nobody," answered Doll, in a quaintly solemn voice, "'cause she's dead."

"No one knows how completely or incompletely we may be severed from consciousness of our old selves, or from interest in our old happinesses, and pursuits, and miseries. I can fancy a fellow being pretty restless in Hades if he left everybody that he knew and was fond of behind him, and felt sorry for his mouldering body that he had been obliged reluctantly to abandon," said Bertie to his cousin.

Clemence turned to Doll. " You must not think of your mother as being under the mould in the churchyard yonder ; you must think of her near you, in the room with you, with very loving and living eyes fixed on you. Eyes that can see far more clearly than ours—mine, Mr. Bertie's, and yours—are able to do. The thought need never frighten you—it would not, would it, Doll ?"

Doll shook her head. " But rather make you feel safe and happy."

Doll looked struck by the suggestion, but there was a dismalness about the corners of her mouth that warned Clemence to discontinue the subject ; feeling sure, however, that she would not forget what had been said to her, and that in lonely hours the thought of her dead mother would come to her.

She chose for her topic now the one dearest to Doll's heart—the horse. She related to two very appreciative listeners how the mare Moonshine allowed the stable cat's kitten to sleep upon her blanketed back. Of how a pony in Canada, whose master (a clergyman) was freezing to death in the sleigh to which the pony was attached, had gone of his own free will and accord—for the reins fell slack from his driver's powerless hands—to a house by the roadside where he had once before been, and neighing loudly, thereby saved his master's life, for they came out to his assistance, and finding the good parson livid and senseless, plunged him into the great hogshead of water standing within the kitchen door, and thus restored him to life and consciousness.

And to her full clear voice, and simple words, the mill-stream sang an accompaniment, and her honest gray eyes only lifted themselves to meet the loving gray ones of

Bertie, and the rapt brown ones of her little nursling, friend, and pupil.

Clemence in her lifetime had had hardly any other but that pitiable part of foil, receptacle of disagreeables suffered, or triumphs enjoyed. She had always had driven home to her by Angela a sense of being older, plainer, and altogether of very common household stuff, compared with that rare bit of Azulejo herself.

Her pride in her sister, and affection for her, had saved her from being either embittered or hardened. Angela's frail beauty and erratic shallow cleverness, seemed to her gifts which every member of a family should be proud for one of its number to possess, feeling no rancour that their special self had not been the favoured one.

Angela, as a child, had always been shod in blue shoes by an adoring father when she was dressed for the afternoon; Clemence had never been the wearer of anything more fantastic than those quaint, ugly little black shoes that are called ankleties.

When Angela had been gowned in pure white to go down to dessert, Clemence had had striped and spotted gowns which had once belonged to her mother, and which hung upon little shoulders that were very dark and scraggy then.   Angela had all her life been white as that maiden of fairy tale, whom the sun bleached like spun cloth, until no white wax could rival her.

The earnest attention which she always received from Bertie, was a delightful novelty to Clemence, and had that effect upon her which it is a pity is not oftener caused—of making her always desire to say something worth the hearing.

Even Doll's delight in her very simple discourse was grateful to her, and an incentive.

"You will come again to-morrow, early, early?" said Doll, touching her dress timidly as she rose up to go.

"By eleven I shall be here," answered Clemence kindly, and laying two ungloved fingers against Doll's velvet cheek as she spoke. "Good-bye, Doll."

"Good-bye to you, Doll," said Bertie also; "you have picked up amazingly, 'pon my word."

Doll stood up on her two somewhat tottering legs to drop a little curtsey, and say with grateful reverence, "Good-bye ma'am good-bye sir," with never a stop between.

They gave her another smile and farewell nod, and went out of the cottage together, crossed the causeway over the stream, and went up the lane into the road that should take them home.

Doll, walking feebly to the door, watched them as far as she could see them; two tall figures with heads that inclined ever so slightly towards one another; a dress that swept neglected; a walking-stick that trailed. They walked on through the midsummer sunshine, between the hedgerows, over waving shadows, out into the glare again, over the green ruts where the daisies, keeping their dainty pink for the stunted dry grasses to look at, turned their pale, pale faces up to the bold, bright sunlight.

END OF VOL. I.

BILLING, PRINTER, GUILDFORD, SURREY.